Shades of Souls Passed

Shades of Souls Passed

True Accounts of Ghostly Encounters in Madison County, New York

By Teresa Andrews

Illustrated by Jacqueline Andrews

ISBN 978-0-557-74024-6

Author's Note

I would like to thank each of my storytellers for sharing their intimate stories with me and making me a believer. I hope that I have done their stories justice.

I would also like to thank Jay, my daughters, and my sister Mary, without whom I could never have pulled this book together.

TABLE OF CONTENTS

Thanksgiving Weekend *(Phil's Story)* 1

Alley-Oop *(Darlene's Story)* 13

Dark Night of the Soul *(Brother Michael's Story)* 21

Hide and Seek *(Mike's Story)* 31

The Midnight Gardener *(Eve's Story)* 43

The Bonnie Brae Loch *(Mary's Story)* 51

Winter Storm *(Danny's Story)* 61

The Meadow *(Tim's Story)* 67

An Unexpected Guest *(Robyn's Story)* 75

Introduction

I grew up in a big old house on a hill that positively begged for the supernatural. Rich in history and nestled in a romantic setting, it was fully equipped with secret passages, dark corners, and a cranky old furnace that could have accounted for many a bump in the night. The attic on the third floor had wide-plank floors that complained most emphatically when you stepped on the wrong one and cedar closets that smelled of mothballs, taffeta, and wool. It all seemed the perfect breeding ground for those moody and restless spirits who were trapped between this world and the next.

Being the youngest of a large and rather imaginative family of seven, I was a fresh canvas upon which my older siblings could paint their magic. I'm sure I learned of the various spirits, or shades as my Aunt Dora called them, that haunted our house before I learned the alphabet. And it wasn't just my brothers and sisters who initiated me into the wonderful, whispering world of ghosts. It was the *well-spirited* adults as well.

I remember the old summer cookouts with innumerable aunts, uncles, and cousins swarming all over the place. We kids would busy ourselves with Kick the Can or Capture the Flag while the parents enjoyed their cocktails and did whatever it is that parents do. Then we'd be called in for hamburgers and hotdogs fresh off the grill. But it was after dinner, after nightfall that the real fun would start. Aunt Dos, Aunt Dora, or Uncle Bill would gather all the kids around them with only the stars and the fireflies to light up their faces. We would listen, holding our breath so as not to miss a single, solitary word of the newest and scariest story yet. I can still feel the surge of ghostly glee when they would tell their tales. I can smell the clean night air, the coffee, and the dying coals in the grill. I hear the faint clinking of dishes being cleaned up in the kitchen.

After the story was over, we were always met with a challenge. There were evil spirits in closets that needed exorcising with a candle and rosary beads. There were ghosts trapped in the basement needing to be set free by some valiant sucker—usually it was me. There was one particular ghost named Admiral Pine who haunted our attic. This poor soul, bound with heavy chains attached to his feet, was big, strong, and had a nasty temper. Apparently, there was a good reason he was chained up. I remember he occasionally needed food to keep him from getting too angry—angry enough to break the chains. Suffice it to say, the possibility that the spirits of the dead lingered in the empty spaces of our world was a continuous thread that wove itself throughout our entire childhood.

But somewhere between Kick the Can and Spin the Bottle, I began to suspect that the ghosts of my youth were nothing more than the fruit of some wonderfully prolific imaginations. At first, I held on to the hope that, even though I had never seen one, spirits still existed … just not in my house. I even made a pact with my favorite aunt, Aunt Dos. We swore that whoever died first would come back and prove once and for all that ghosts can exist.

Well, she died first. In fact, it was not too long after that conversation, and she never came back to me in any way, shape, form, or manner. I waited patiently for a couple of years, but that little seed of skepticism had planted itself inside of me, and I eventually decided that there was no such thing as ghosts. The people who claimed to have seen them simply had to have been, at best, sadly mistaken.

Although I didn't admit it at the time I began researching for this book, I was going into it with more of a skeptical approach than I had intended. I was sure that I would leave most of the interviews thinking that someone should be seeing a therapist.

Yet when I began to hear the firsthand accounts in this book, my skin really started to crawl again like it did when I was a kid. I felt the doors slowly creak open with every tale I heard. That wonder and spine-chilling delight returned, and I found myself right back at those picnics with the fireflies, the crickets, and the crackling sensation of a world much bigger, much richer than what can be seen.

Let me assure you that the men and women who so kindly shared their extraordinary experiences with me are not attention seekers with overactive imaginations. They aren't people who even *wanted* a visit from the other side. They were not looking for a life-altering experience. They're just perfectly ordinary people who were simply going about their daily lives until one day—or night as the case may be—they were met with the stunning realization that sometimes our world very definitely intersects with the world of spirits.

All of my leads on this project came by word of mouth, as I wanted the stories to be both fresh and personal. I want to thank each and every one of my storytellers for sharing their very intimate experiences with me. For some, and for various reasons, it wasn't easy. I have changed the names and locations of some of the stories to protect the privacy of the people involved—those who have passed on as well as those who have not.

So pull the covers up over your head on this dark and stormy night. Switch on the flashlight, and begin your journey into the unseen spaces—the spaces where the souls of shades passed reside. Be sure to gather your courage and keep your wits about you because I assure you, you're not the only one in your bedroom tonight!

Chapter One

Thanksgiving Weekend

Phil's Story

It was dark as the plane slowly taxied its way to the terminal. The lights outside glared off the wet tarmac, creating an eerie sort of loneliness. It had been a long trip, and Phil was tired. He'd stayed up most of the night before finishing up a paper on stem cell research and had only gotten a couple hours of sleep before he had to catch his flight to Syracuse. He didn't want to worry about studying, papers, or tests this weekend; he wanted to relax and enjoy Thanksgiving weekend with his mother at her new home in Upstate New York.

It had been over six months since he'd seen her, and it had been a wild year for both of them. Phil's father had died suddenly and prematurely just over a year ago, and in less time than it takes to make a pot of coffee, their neat, predictable lives had become a veritable mountain of change and challenge. Phil's mom needed to get away and start fresh. So she sold her home in Madison, Wisconsin, got a position as Dean of Administration at Morrisville College, and moved to Hamilton, New York. Phil leaned his head against the small, oval window and sighed. They had a lot to talk about.

Inside, the lights remained dimmed, and even though the flight was full, a restless silence filled the cabin as the 727 finally rounded the last corner to the terminal. A pretty voice came over the loudspeaker and politely reminded the passengers to keep their seatbelts fastened and remain seated until the plane came to a complete stop. The battle-weary travelers acquiesced, but the instant the plane stopped and the lights dinged on, there was a mad flurry of arms, legs, bags, and coats, and within a matter of seconds, the aisle became nothing less than a Milwaukee traffic jam.

Inside the terminal, it was bustling with Thanksgiving homecomings, but Phil spotted his mother's tall, slim figure immediately.

He was relieved, but not surprised to see that she looked great! She was dressed to the nines in a long gray sweater-coat with a red cashmere scarf wrapped around her neck. Her long black hair only served to highlight her dark brown eyes, and the smile of pride that she greeted him with was, as always, enough to make Phil believe he could do anything. It felt good to wrap her in his arms and give her a long squeeze, and he could tell the feeling was mutual.

It was snowing outside. The fields that surrounded Route 81 were brushed with white, but the roads were dark and wet. His mom maneuvered her Mercedes expertly through the Syracuse traffic like she'd lived in the area her whole life. It was late, so they stopped at the Scotch and Sirloin for something to eat, whereupon she filled him in on the weekend's festivities. Tomorrow, the Rochester relatives were coming for Thanksgiving dinner. And on Friday, she was hosting an open house for her new neighbors and co-workers. *Yeah*, Phil smiled as he thought to himself; *she's doing just fine.*

They covered the basics of each other's lives over an after-dinner cup of coffee, then headed east on Route 92. By the time they hit Route 20, there was barely any traffic, barely any lights, and the roads were covered with snow. They climbed up long hills that seemed to go on forever like the slow rise of a rollercoaster. It was so remote and dark that, when they reached the tops, Phil thought they might drop off the face of the earth. But then, after winding down the other side, a little hamlet would glow through the darkness like a cluster of diamonds in the snow.

"Good Lord, Mrs. H," he chided playfully, "Where are you taking me?"

His mother smiled, "You'll see."

It was just before eleven when they drove into Hamilton, and the tiny village seemed to materialize out of nowhere. Two blocks of brick buildings that seemed ridiculously tall for their relative space loomed over one very confusing five-way intersection. And that seemed to be the extent of it. Phil spotted a restaurant, a bank, and a small convenience store, but all were closed for the evening, and it gave him the feeling that they were driving through an abandoned Hollywood set. He knew that Hamilton was home to the esteemed Colgate University, but *holy cow*, Phil thought to himself; his mother must have really needed a change!

It had stopped snowing by the time they turned left at the intersection onto Madison Street. The houses were all large and dark inside except for a few dimly lit windows and the occasional blue flicker of a television set. Barren maple trees loomed over either side of the road like snow-covered skeletons. When his mother turned into the driveway of her new home, Phil got out of the car, stretched his head back as far as it could go, and looked up at the house in disbelief.

"Oh my God, mother! What possessed you? It looks like The Addam's Family house!"

The house had obviously seen better days, and those were probably more than a century ago. The faded white front porch and peeling paint only whispered of the grace and dignity it surely once possessed. But what struck Phil the most about it was that it was the tallest, narrowest house he had ever seen. And like everything else he'd seen so far, it seemed completely disproportionate. It was a federal style house with a flat roof. The first floor had two tall windows that were the same size as the front door to their right. The second story had three medium sized windows, and the third three tiny windows. All of this added to the vertical effect, and Phil almost felt dizzy looking up at it. All in all, this ramshackle old monster of a house couldn't possibly be more different from the contemporary homes that his mother had always lived in.

"What were you thinking?" He continued as she led the way through the front door. "You all alone in a big old haunted house like this?"

"I know, I know," she said with a warm, but defiant smile. "Just wait until you see the inside before you cast any aspersions on my sanity." Then, taking his hand, she whisked him through the foyer and into the front hall.

She was right. It was just as warm and cozy inside as it was grim and bleak on the outside. She had stripped the place and renovated everything from top to bottom. Glistening hardwood floors and oriental rugs stretched throughout the entire downstairs. The walls had been freshly painted with rich, earthy colors, and the old fashioned trim around the doors and windows shone like glossy pearl. The furniture was an eclectic mix of antique and comfortable, with sparkling crystal sconces and porcelain lamps leaving no corner unlit. A slow burning fire in the living room hearth cast a welcoming glow on the velvet chairs and couch that surrounded it. And to complete the ambiance, the house smelled of a full days worth of baking. Phil felt like he had just walked into a Hallmark greeting card. She saw the expression on his face and laughed.

"I told you so," she almost gloated. "It's been very therapeutic for me. Now, come with me. I'll show you your room, and then we can settle in by the fire and do some more catching up."

She led the way up an immaculately restored staircase that was as long as it was steep. Perfectly centered at the top was a tall, arched window that, once again, seemed to amplify the narrowness of the house.

"You know," she said as she neared the top, "speaking of haunted houses, we just might actually have a ghost in residence here." She turned and raised her brows so the whites of her eyes shimmered in the shadows.

"Oh really," Phil responded in kind. "And who might that be?" He didn't believe in ghosts any more than she did, but joined the fun and played along.

She turned and continued down the hallway, the heels of her boots clicking steadily. Phil counted the doorways as he followed her to the bedroom she had prepared for him. Six bedrooms!

"Why, Colonel Eaton, that's who." She never stopped talking as she fussed about, giving the final touches to the perfectly appointed room. "The first time I heard about him was from the woman who owned this house before me." Phil watched as she drew the quilted bedspread back and folded it with deft precision. "She was showing me the house," she continued as she patted and primped the fluffy pillows. "And when we were in the basement, she showed me a door. She told me that, in order to keep her children from wandering, she always told them to stay away from that door and never, under any circumstances, are they to open it."

She picked up a small vase of flowers on the bedside table and returned it to the exact same spot. Then, after scanning the room with a critical eye, she turned to Phil with a mischievously ominous smile, "Because if they did," her eyes glowed like burning coals, "the ghost of Colonel Eaton would get out!"

Phil laughed as they headed back downstairs. "And who was this Colonel Eaton? Did he live here?"

"I don't think he lived in this house, but I don't know. He was an elderly man who must have lived somewhere around here. Old Miss Driscoll, who lives two doors down, said she remembered that when she was a little girl, he used to stand on the corner and give nickels and dimes to all the children that passed."

"Hmm," Phil muttered. Then, lowering his voice to almost a whisper, he used his most dramatic voice. "Have *you* seen or heard anything of the Colonel?"

"Good heavens, no! You know I don't believe in that nonsense!"

They both laughed as she led the way into the kitchen and poured some hot tea. Within minutes they were comfortably seated on either side of the living room couch, she with her boots off and feet up. The wood crackled slowly in the hearth, and the reflection of the flames danced about the floor. There was a comfortable silence as they both relaxed into their space. They would be up for another hour or so talking about his schoolwork, her new job, and surely they would shed some tears over the loss of his dad. But there was something Phil wanted to say before they even got started.

"By the way, mom, your house looks beautiful."

Phil woke up to the unmistakable aroma of roast turkey and oyster stuffing. He inhaled deeply and let out a low, anticipatory growl. He'd been thinking about his mother's turkey dinner for weeks, and now that it was only hours away, he almost felt like he could drool.

He looked at his watch. It was nine thirty. Even though he'd been exhausted when he'd gone to bed last night, he hadn't slept well. Unfamiliar surroundings always threw a wrench into his sleep for the first night or two. His mother would expect him to sleep in, and his body was complaining, but Phil pulled himself out of bed, threw on a sweatshirt, and followed the smell of the turkey.

Even though she was just one woman, the kitchen was abuzz with activity. Culinary accoutrements in all sizes and shapes covered every square inch of counter space, and the room smelled like heaven. Over on a table under the window, a light cloud of steam curling up from a pot of fresh coffee caught his attention. His mother looked up at him and smiled. "I have some fresh pastries and juice for you when you're ready."

She hadn't looked this happy in a long time. Like she always said, this was her thing.

"Zeola and crew will be here around one o'clock," she announced, "and we will have dinner at three. Do you think you could bring in some wood for the fire? It's out in the garage. And then I need you to …"

Phil came over and gave her a kiss on the forehead, and at the same time snuck his hand behind her toward a plate of stuffed olives.

But she was too quick for him. Giving his hand a perfunctory slap, she nudged him back toward the coffee and pastries.

"That's for later, young man," she scolded. "Now you sit there, eat your breakfast, and keep me company while I cook!"

Phil breathed deep into his belly then let out a long sigh, "Ah … it's good to be home."

The day went without a hitch. Zeola, Maxine, Scott, and a whole slew of little cousins that Phil had never even seen before arrived promptly at one, and the noise level never dipped below a roar until after dessert. Somewhere in between the champagne with fresh strawberries and shrimp cocktail, Phil found himself momentarily unoccupied and decided he needed to scratch an itch that he'd had ever since his first cup off coffee—the door in the cellar.

Without telling his mother, he slipped unnoticed through the basement door and flicked on the light switch. It was awkward going down the stairs. He had to lean down in order to not hit his head, and the steps were so narrow he had to place his large feet sideways. The floor was mostly earth except for a slab of cement underneath the furnace and water heater. A single bulb hanging from the ceiling offered only the dimmest of light, but he could see the door the instant he reached the bottom of the stairs.

He walked over to it carefully avoiding the cobwebs that hung from the pipes. It must have been an outdoor entrance to the basement at one time, but judging from the thud when he banged on it, the bulkhead had been filled in from the other side at some point. Phil shrugged. "No big deal. Just looks like your garden variety door to me," he said to himself, then climbed back up the stairs just in time for dinner.

The following day was equally busy. It seemed as though they had just finished cleaning up from the night before when they had to start preparing for the open house. But Phil's mom had everything organized right down to an embroidery-covered guest book on a table just outside the foyer. For two hours, the smell of cinnamon and roasted chestnuts filled the downstairs as new friends, neighbors, and co-workers poured through the front door oohing and aahing over the improvements to the house.

When the last guest had left, Phil's mother let out a contented sigh, retrieved the guest book, and sat down next to the fire. She smiled as she slowly passed her forefinger through the pages of names and offered interesting side comments about some of the more illustrious guests. Just as she was about to verify that Phil had met the president of Morrisville College, she stopped short and caught her breath.

"What's this?" she said with her finger stopped at one of the names. Her mouth hung open and, for an instant, she looked completely nonplussed.

"What?" Phil tried to keep a serious face.

"Why, somebody signed 'Colonel Eaton!' Who do you think …?"

Then she looked up at Phil, and he saw the bewilderment on her face melt to the smile of a little girl. "Oh you devil!"

"Gotcha!" Phil threw his head back and let out a series of wildly self-satisfied whoops.

His mother joined him but chimed in, "Only for a second, you scallywag."

The following day, a pale November sun streamed through the windows and cast long narrow beams of light across the hardwood floors. Outside, the snow was melting fast and dazzling little beads of water clung precariously to the branches above them. It was his final day of vacation, and Phil wanted to soak up the leisure and comforts of home as much as he could before he headed back to fourteen-hour days of lectures, classes, and studying. He and his mother went for a leisurely walk around the village in the morning, had leftovers for lunch, and then went for a drive in the countryside. It was just what he needed.

At three o'clock in the afternoon, Phil's mother had to go to a tea that her department was hosting. Phil fidgeted around a bit, then decided to light a fire and take a nap. He stretched out on the couch, pulled an afghan up around himself, and listened to the crackling of the fire. But sleep eluded him. A little past four, he looked at his watch and gave up. Actually, a cup of tea sounded good right now. He wandered into the kitchen and looked out the window over the sink as he filled the kettle with water. It was dusk, and the last remaining light of the day cast a pale lavender hue over the stones in the garden out back.

Just as he turned to bring the kettle to the stove, Phil felt an ice-cold shaft of wind pass right through him. It was as if he had walked in front of an open door in an arctic blizzard. He was startled, but brushed it off as a typical feature of a drafty old house. He put the kettle on the stove and walked back a couple of steps to where he felt it, and again, there was an obvious change of temperature. It didn't make any sense. Just as he started looking around for an open window or a crack in the foundation, he heard what sounded like pieces of metal sporadically falling on the hardwood floor upstairs.

"What the hell?" He looked out toward the front hall. What was that sound? He knew that he had heard it somewhere before, but his brain was struggling to remember where. He inched quietly into the front hall, alongside the staircase, listening. Then, just as he heard it again right over his head at the top of the stairs, he recognized it. It was the sound of coins falling to the floor and the vibrating hum as they spiraled to a stop.

Phil thought for a moment that someone must have snuck into the house and was playing games with him. Either that or a clumsy thief had broken in and knocked some change off a table. A rush of adrenaline surged through him as he rounded the bottom of the staircase to confront the mysterious prowler. But when he looked up, he saw something so unnerving, so unfathomable, that he stopped dead where he stood and was amazed to hear himself gasp.

There, at the top of the stairs stood a form, a shape, a thing. Phil didn't know what to call it. His eyes, his brain couldn't even process it. Everything he had ever learned about living and nonliving matter, everything he had known or even imagined about life, death, or anything in between, all of that evaporated in an instant, disappeared like a puff of smoke.

It had no clearly defined outline or features, yet its overall shape resembled that of tall man. The substance was gray, but intangible, more like a dark shadow than anything else. Yet it was solid enough that he couldn't see through it; the form was enough to block the fading light from the window at the top of the stairs. Phil was both mesmerized and terrified, more terrified than he had ever been in his life—not because he felt any danger or malice from this dark specter, but because there is nothing more terrifying to a man of science than something that is indefinable, immeasurable, and incomprehensible.

After several moments, Phil instinctively moved back a step and to his complete horror, the figure at the top of the stairs moved down a step and then stopped. Phil couldn't believe it! Was it a mirage, a trick of the light? He took another step backwards, and just as he did, the figure moved just that much closer. This was too much. Every nerve in Phil's body jumped to attention.

Once again, Phil moved back another step and, once again, the figure moved toward him. There was a part of him that was so fascinated by this anomaly that he wanted to investigate, but there was a bigger part of him that wanted to turn and run like a scared rabbit. He couldn't do either. He could barely feel his limbs. The thought of turning his back on the thing and having it chase him was too much for him to bear.

Slowly, step-by-step, Phil walked backwards around the stairwell toward the kitchen. Sure enough, the ghostly figure followed suit and, with horrifying precision, descended the staircase at exactly the same pace as Phil. At one point Phil was beside it and saw that there was nothing behind it. This inexplicable figure of gray was neither liquid, solid, nor gas, but it was definitely some sort of entity. *What the hell was it?*

Never taking his eyes off his dogged pursuer, Phil backed his way into the kitchen, his hands groping for something to guide him. The figure followed, keeping a steady distance between them. Just as Phil was backed up into the counter, waiting for the inevitable confrontation, the damned thing passed right by the kitchen and turned toward the cellar door instead. It took a couple of seconds for Phil to pull his stomach back down his throat. Then, anchoring his hands to the counter behind him, he leaned over and peeked around the corner. Right before his eyes, the ghostly prowler passed straight through the closed cellar door.

Phil felt an overwhelming combination of terror and awe. He wasn't even sure if he could convince his legs to move, but he knew that he had to go into the basement. He stood frozen for several moments in an effort to regroup his senses that seemed to have splattered all over the floor. He then made his way over to the cellar door and slowly turned the knob. His hands were wet with sweat. Silently, he pushed the door open. The light from outside had faded to practically nothing and the basement was as dark as a tomb. Phil took a deep breath and held it. Using every ounce of whatever courage he still possessed, he reached his arm up through the cobwebs and flicked on the light. Lowering his head and steadying himself with his hands against the wall, he carefully crept down four of the narrow steps. Instead of going further, he leaned forward and looked into the depths of the basement. For some reason his eyes went right to the door across the way, Colonel Eaton's door. The massive cloud of gray was heading right for the door, but before Phil could see it go through, it vanished. There was nothing.

Just then, as Phil stood there stooped over on the stairs trying to make sense of everything, anything really, he heard that sound again; the sound of coins being dropped on the bare floor upstairs. He felt like he was losing his mind! If he stayed there for another minute he could very well do just that. Without a moment's hesitation, he turned back up the cellar stairs, shut the light off, and closed the door. He went directly past the stairwell to the front door, grabbed his coat and got out of the house.

Phil must have walked around the village for over an hour before he could even begin to steady his nerves. It was dark, and thankfully, a brisk wind slapped him upside the face like the hero in an old black and white movie. How could this have happened? It didn't make sense. He was a man of logic, a man who spurned superstition and stories of ghostly encounters. If he couldn't see it, hear it, touch it, then, no matter how convincing, it didn't exist. But he did see it, he heard it, and, God knows, he felt it.

Phil and his mother ate out that night, but Phil consumed more wine than he did food. He knew his mother would laugh when he told her about his afternoon, and she did. He couldn't hold it against her; he would have done the same thing had their roles been reversed. So he played it down and didn't make a big deal about it. When they got back to the house, there was no lingering sense of what had happened earlier. It seemed to be just the unusually tall, narrow house that it was. Nevertheless, Phil slept on the couch by the fire that night instead of in his bedroom. In fact, he didn't even go upstairs until late the following morning when he had to pack his belongings for the trip back to Milwaukee. As he climbed the stairs, he could feel his nerves grow taut as he waited to see if he would feel something, but he didn't. And when he reached the top landing, he couldn't help but look to see if there were any nickels or dimes on the floor. He wasn't sure if he was relieved or not, but there were none.

As he sat on the plane waiting for take-off, Phil rested his head on the soft little pillow the airline had provided and closed his eyes. He thought of that peculiarly tall, narrow house in that even more peculiar little town of Hamilton. Festive images of the parties, the walks, and the cozy late-night talks competed unsuccessfully for space with the unforgettable picture of that figure on the stairs and the sound of falling coins. They were permanently etched into his mind, and he knew, no matter how hard he tried, he would never be able to come up with a logical explanation. As much as that bothered his innate sense of logic, he realized he just had to learn to live with it. But one thing he could say with concrete certainty; he would miss his mother, but he certainly wasn't going to miss that house. Milwaukee was looking good right now and, much to Phil's surprise, so were the books, the papers, and the lectures.

The lights in the cabin dimmed and the plane started to accelerate for take off. Once it got into the air, Phil took a deep breath, shifted his long legs around as best he could, and prepared to go to sleep. Just as he felt his body start to sink into dreamland, he saw his mother's warm smile as she gave him a good-bye hug at the airport. She was reminding him to work hard, eat right, get enough rest, and all the other things mothers like to worry about. When she was done and Phil had turned to go to his gate, she reached up and stopped him.

"Oh and Phil," she said, "One last thing …"

Phil rolled his eyes with affection and turned to her. "Yes mother?"

"If I ever do see Colonel Eaton, I'll make sure to tell him you said hello!"

Chapter Two

Alley-Oop

Darlene's Story

A red-tailed hawk sat perched atop a craggy old maple tree, his shrewd, wizened eyes surveying all that lay above and beneath him. The late afternoon sky was warm and blue. Acres and acres of lush green fields stretched as far as the eye could see, and the earth was quiet and still, waiting for evening's approach. June had come as she had so many times before, and covered the fields of Clockville with her luxurious mantle, leaving the endless landscape a perfect picture of bucolic bliss.

But there was something drastically different about this particular afternoon. Something so quiet, so infinitely subtle, yet so powerful that the very earth seemed to tremble from the force of it.

On the top of a hill in the middle of a patchwork of fields stood a small stand of trees, whose ghostly limbs broke the otherwise unobstructed horizon. At the base of the trees was a scattering of large rocks. Just fifteen yards to the north of those boulders was a large, newly filled grave, invisible to everything except the sky above. The soil was still soft and cool to the touch, and the only sound that broke the silence was the faint rustling of the wind coming over the grass.

It was here that Darlene lay—prostrate, on top of the grave, the side of her face pressed against the dirt, her arms outstretched in the form of an embrace. It was as though a tremendous gravitational force was pulling her through the eight feet of earth that separated her from the one thing she needed, the only thing she couldn't live without. She was alone now, more alone than she had ever been in her life. And every living thing, even the slightest blade of grass, watched as she clung to the mound of dirt and sang a silent requiem.

She had thought about this moment the whole trip home. Kevin, her farmhand, had known that she would want some time alone, so he had helped her get the horses into the barn, then left her to grieve the loss of the horse she'd left behind. He knew that Alley Oop was more than a world-class champion to Darlene. But he couldn't begin to fathom the loss that she felt right now. Alley Oop was her best friend, her better half, her partner, her soul mate, and the only constant thing she'd ever had in her whole life. And now, just eight feet away from her, but unreachable, she could never touch him again. How could she say goodbye? He was truly a part of her, every bit as much as her arms or her legs. Even deeper than that, he was her very heart. How could she go on living without her heart?

Darlene squeezed the earth tighter as she remembered the feel of his soft muzzle and warm breath against her cheek, his strong neck when he would turn around and hug her with it, and his distinctive knicker that he always greeted her with when she came into the barn.

* * *

She was in her twenties and a little green around the collar when she first met Alley Oop. He was a six-year-old giant of a horse that had all the strength and power it took to be a champion jumper except for one thing … no one could ride him.

At the time, she was training in Denver with a man named Wilson Dennehey. He was a short man with salt and pepper hair and hands as big as a grizzly's. He'd been in the business for years and could spot a championship horse a mile away. It was Wilson who told her about Alley Oop.

"I saw a horse in New York two years ago. He was a beauty. But unless he has settled down, there's no way a little thing like you could ride him."

Darlene always wondered if Wilson was just baiting her, and if his challenge had received its desired effect. It didn't really matter. They were in New York the following weekend.

She remembered the first time she saw Alley Oop being led out of the barn. God, he was beautiful. The minute she laid eyes on him, Darlene knew he was something special. He was a chestnut Belgian Warm blood more than sixteen hands and 1,500 pounds of sheer muscle. It was all she could do to stay on him, but she had never felt such energy, such power between her legs.

She couldn't help but smile through her tears when she remembered how he bucked. It wasn't like anything she'd seen before or since. He would jump four feet straight up into the air, and *then* raise his forelegs. But even back then, she instinctively knew that he wasn't trying to be naughty. He just had too much energy and needed someone to show him what to do with it. They were two of a kind. Together, and only together, they would be champs. Wilson disagreed and did everything he could to talk her out of it. But she went with her gut. She bought him in 1989.

They started winning right away. To the amazement of everyone except Darlene, Alley Oop performed beautifully, and like she'd expected, he loved his job every bit as much as she did. Nothing could beat the rush they both felt when they would soar over the flowered fence posts. He would clear any jump by more than a foot, tucking his front legs as tight as a knot, and stretching his hind legs back until just the right moment.

The next ten years of Darlene and Alley Oop's career were filled with ribbons, unbelievable opportunities, and open ended offers from all over the world to buy Alley Oop. But Darlene wouldn't even think of selling. For it was after the noise and excitement of the competition, in the quiet stillness of the barn, that Alley Oop was her real champion. Like anyone else, Darlene wasn't spared the personal struggles of life, and when she felt like she was going to crumble, she would go to him. She would talk to him, tell him things she would never tell another soul. Alley Oop would turn his head back to her and affectionately nibble and sniff her hair. His wordless devotion was something she couldn't part with, not for all the money in the world. Even after she retired him and bought the farm on Cottons Road in Clockville, she put him in the first stall on the corner so that he would be the first thing she saw when she came into the barn. They had a commitment to each other right from the very beginning. She wouldn't falter, and neither would he.

But had she faltered? Had she let Alley Oop down? Should she have done something different? When Kevin called yesterday afternoon and told her that Alley Oop was acting strange, she was afraid that it was another bout of colic. She would have come home immediately, but that was impossible. Her truck had broken down and she couldn't leave the other horses stranded and unattended at the show grounds. She tried to be optimistic and hoped it would turn out to be nothing. But the fear that had slowly crept its way inside her was like the first tiny, almost imperceptible drop of rain that would turn out to be a torrential flood.

Kevin called again later in the night to tell her that the vet confirmed it was colic, and Alley Oop was getting worse. When he asked for permission to put him down, Darlene felt like her breath was being sucked out of her.

"No," she said, "I'll get there as soon as possible."

She sat up most of the night crippled with fear and guilt. Was she just being stubborn again? Was she being selfish in letting Alley Oop suffer just so she didn't have to suffer the loss of him? Or would Alley Oop want to fight his way through it like he did three years ago? She had been stubborn then too, but it had worked. The surgeons took out twenty-five feet of his intestines and told her it was amazing he was still alive. It was a long recovery, but Darlene was at his side every step of the way, and they beat it. Why couldn't they do it again?

But Kevin's call at six o'clock that morning had changed everything. She had gotten the truck fixed and was getting ready to pack up when her cell phone rang. She was standing just outside the barn. She would never forget it.

"Darlene, you've got to let us put him to sleep."

His words pounded into her brain like an ice pick. She felt like she was going to explode. This couldn't be happening! She couldn't see, she couldn't hear. Her mouth and throat instantly became so dry she could barely scrape the words out of her mouth. "Can't you wait until I get there?"

"No. He's trying to roll in his stall." Kevin's voice was pleading, but firm. "There's nothing we can do, Darlene. He's in horrible pain. You can't let him suffer."

The picture of her Alley Oop writhing in pain was more than she could bear. God, she needed to be with him, and she knew that he would want her there. But there was too much time and space between them. Every minute she took to get to him was another minute of agony for the one she had vowed to protect. It was the hardest thing she would ever do. It felt as if she took a machete and cut her self straight down the center.

"You're right, Kevin … you have my permission to put him to sleep."

* * *

Darlene lifted her head off the soil and looked up at the deep periwinkle sky. The sun had set, but there weren't any stars out yet.

She'd lost all track of time. Her two dogs, Lola and Luna, were lying under the stand of trees waiting for her. They were probably hungry hours ago, but hadn't complained. They knew something was different. But she couldn't leave Alley Oop now. She had broken their contract last night. She hadn't been there for him, and this was the closest she would ever be to him again. She had to stay … just a little while longer.

She laid her head down again and rubbed her hands through the soil. If only she could touch him, smell him; hear him just one more time. If only she'd had the chance to say goodbye. No, that wasn't true. It wouldn't help. She couldn't say goodbye last night, and she probably never would. It just wasn't possible. Kevin had called her on her way home and asked her if she wanted him to bury Alley Oop before she arrived.

"Bury him on the hill by the trees," she had answered.

And she was glad that she had. The thought of seeing his lifeless body made her sick to her stomach. She couldn't have that image even enter her consciousness. Then it would be too real. She would have to admit that he was gone forever, and that was too much to take in. She could only allow that truth to enter one horrifying little piece at a time.

Finally, she pulled her exhausted body up from the ground. She was covered with dirt from head to toe and could barely walk. Night had fallen and everything was dark. Her eyes were almost swollen shut, but she could see a half moon dangling just above the woods to the south, and the air smelled cool and sweet. It occurred to her as she walked down the hill toward the house that she would normally have thought it was a beautiful night and would have been glad to be home. But the house was dark and empty, and the big red barn looked like a giant tomb. The earth had changed somehow. It all seemed incongruous, even ugly now, and it certainly didn't feel like home.

She was so tired, so numb that she almost forgot to go into the barn for night check. But Lola and Luna trotted happily toward the side door of the barn, just like they had every night for years. All Darlene wanted to do was head directly to her bed and disappear for however long it took. But instead, she followed her dogs across the gravel driveway to the tack room door, where they waited with their tails wagging.

She didn't turn the lights on. She didn't want to disturb the horses, and the red glow of the emergency light was enough for them to make their way. Besides, she could do night check blindfolded if she had to. In fact, in one very real sense, she was. As she made her way through the tack room and down the hallway to the barn aisle, she didn't notice the pale shafts of moonlight coming in through the barred windows or the sound of her rubber soled boots on the wood floors like she always did. She didn't breathe in the smell of clean leather and fresh hay, or feel that particular serenity of a full barn at night. She was just an exhausted, empty shell of a woman whose insides had died fifteen hours before, who was merely operating on automatic pilot.

Even as she approached Alley Oop's empty corner stall, the first stall she would pass, she was oblivious. She didn't even fear the emptiness of the space that once held the one true thing in her life. She didn't fear anything. She rounded the corner like a zombie. But then she heard it.

It wasn't loud or spectacular. The skies didn't open up and send forth a magnificent beam of light to overpower her, and the earth didn't shake. It was quiet and warm, as soft and unobtrusive as a kitten rubbing up against your leg. But when she heard it, she dropped straight to the ground like a rag doll, her limbs spewed out on all sides. It was the sound that she had heard every night check for the last eighteen years, a sound she knew as intimately as that of her own breath. She never imagined that she would hear it ever again. It was Alley Oop's distinctive nicker! He was greeting her like he always had when she first came into the barn.

Darlene's heart pounded against her ribs so hard it felt like they would break any minute and a whirr of white noise vibrated through her entire body. Would she see him if she looked up? Would he be standing there with his big head stretched down over the top of his door reaching for her hair with his muzzle? Would there be forgiveness in his eyes? She wanted to stand up and hug him, wrap her arms around his big warm neck and hold on forever. But before she even raised her eyes to look up, she knew it. He was gone.

"No!" she sobbed, "Come back! Don't leave me!"

But he had vanished as quickly as he had come. And she knew that he had come to say goodbye. He was never coming back again. This was a one-time thing. She hadn't wanted to face it. She hadn't been able to. But now she had no choice. She couldn't will her way out of this one. Maybe one day she would see this leave-taking as an extraordinary gift, a perfect testament to Alley Oop's determination and the sacred commitment that they shared. But not now, this was goodbye.

And so she sat there on the cold cement floor, bleached in the pale moonlight. Lola, Luna, and the other horses watched with curious but respectful silence. She was just a speck of a thing compared to the massive barn that surrounded her, and even smaller under the infinite night sky. In a matter of hours, the sun would rise again and a whole world full of people would wake up and go about their day.

But tonight, on a small patch of land in Clockville, New York, the earth would stand watch and wait with her for the night to pass. It would pass, but the earth would never forget. That night was etched in the rings of every tree, the eye of every star, in the very fiber of creation. And it would stay there. Just as the small stand of trees on the hill would remain there long after new grass had covered the mound of dirt, so would that quiet, almost invisible summer night in June.

Chapter Three

Dark Night of the Soul

Brother Michael's Story

A winter storm warning was in effect for the entire Northeast. A travel advisory had been issued. But that didn't stop Brother Michael. He pulled the collar of his overcoat up around his neck and headed out into the cold, damp morning anyway. He didn't have too much faith in the forecasters. They seemed to be wrong more often than right, and even if it were to get as bad as they predicted, he and his trusty old Mercury had traveled over the roads of Route 81 through all sorts of weather. So the threat of a couple of snow squalls didn't worry him one bit.

In fact, there wasn't much that did worry the aging Franciscan. He was an intelligent and logical man, not given to fits of nervousness or apprehension. His decisions were cerebral and analytical rather than instinctual. Even his decision to become a monk had been a logical one. Once he had finally concluded that there was indeed a God, it only made perfect sense to him to devote the rest of his life to Him. Although he truly respected those with a more intuitive and passionate nature, he had come to accept both the gifts and limitations that God had given him. His was a simple life, and he considered himself an ordinary man merely doing God's work.

A sudden, temperamental gust of wind blew his pearl-colored hair straight up and sent his cassock swirling underneath his overcoat. "*Hmm,*" he said with an appreciative smile, "Well done." Then he threw his old leather duffel bag and briefcase in the back seat of his car and, with a quick glance back at the monastery he loved, climbed in. God willing, he would be in Syracuse in just over an hour. That would give him time to have a little lunch and a nice hot cup of tea before he began his three-day conference on the mystery of The Holy Trinity.

An old friend of his had arranged for Brother Michael to stay at a house just outside of Syracuse on Cazenovia Lake. Although the house was generally used only during the summer months, he was assured that it was completely and comfortably furnished and fully winterized. It meant a forty-minute drive, but this pleased Brother Michael because after a busy day of hustle and bustle, he much preferred the solitude and intimacy of a home to a noisy hotel. He was familiar with Cazenovia as well and had a spattering of friends he could call on if he felt the need for company.

By the time he reached St. Mary's Church, more than four inches of snow had fallen on the city of Syracuse, and Brother Michael seriously doubted that anyone would show up for the conference. But, once again, he had underestimated the tenacity of the typical Upstate New Yorker. A good crowd of hardy souls arrived and, at least as far as he could tell, everything went well.

There were several invitations for dinner, of course, but Brother Michael declined. He was tired and wanted to settle in should the storm take a turn for the worse. He thanked everyone for coming, gathered his materials, and headed out to his car. It was four-thirty. The snow had stopped, but a heavy shelf of gray clouds seemed to hover ominously low in the sky. His car looked like a big scoop of ice cream, and he groaned as he remembered that he left his scraper back at the monastery. Brushing off the snow as best he could with his elbows and gloves, he started for Cazenovia.

As he wound his way over the hills of Route 92, it began to get dark, and the snow started up again, but much heavier than before. In fact, if it weren't for the two red taillights on the car ahead of him, he wouldn't have been able to tell the road from the field.

It was then that it occurred to him that he'd never been to Cazenovia during the winter months. He'd remembered it as a little Garden of Eden, with lovely green pastures and a jewel of a lake in the middle. But as he looked out at the sheets of white blowing across the hood of his car, it hardly looked like the same place at all. In fact, he wasn't sure he hadn't fallen off the face of the earth. But he good-heartedly made a sign of the cross, got his bearings, and with more than a little luck, Brother Michael eventually found his destination.

He was grateful to see that the long, narrow driveway leading to the house had been plowed and the sidewalk shoveled. It had obviously snowed plenty since, but the smooth impressions in the snow were enough to show him the way. The porch light had been left on for him, and inside he could see the warm, welcoming glow of a lamp. As he fumbled through his pockets for the house key, he noticed that there were no other house lights or streetlights for as far as he could see. The nearby camps stood dark and empty, like frozen memorials of summers past, while crooked trees and cedar hedges seemed to rise up out of the snow like gargoyles. Thank God he was comfortable with solitude, he thought. For the place felt almost too isolated, too desolate … even for him.

Inside, the house was more than comfortable, as promised, and it was furnished with the lake in mind. The entire east side was made up of a stretch of sliding glass doors facing what he assumed would be the ice-covered lake. A note was left on the kitchen counter welcoming him and explaining the whereabouts of everything he might need. Brother Michael flipped on the outdoor spotlight and looked out at the grounds. The snow had stopped again, and there was nothing between him and the huge, white expanse of the lake. Again he felt a fleeting sensation of complete aloneness, an unfamiliar feeling, as though he were standing on the edge of a huge abyss. He quickly shook it off, turned on the rest of the lights, and found himself something to eat. After going over his notes for the next day and saying his prayers, he went upstairs to bed.

As always, sleep came easily for Brother Michael. And as he slept, a light but steady snowfall continued to cover the house in a silent shroud of white. Somewhere in the middle of the night he was awakened by a loud, roaring sound—a sound that not only startled him, but totally baffled him because it was completely inconsistent with his surroundings. It was the sound of water, a lot of water, crashing water. But it was the dead of winter. He was surrounded by nothing but snow and ice. He had to have been dreaming.

Sitting up, he took a moment to rub his eyes and clear his head. Outside, he could see the snow falling innocently enough, yet inside it sounded like he was standing on the edge of a waterfall. He didn't know what to think! It was too loud to think, and it didn't make any sense at all. The only thing he could come up with was that a major pipe must have burst, and judging from the sound of it, the whole of Cazenovia Lake was exploding into the house. Whatever it was, he knew he had to think and act quickly if he was going to make it out in one piece.

He looked to see if there was a telephone anywhere in the room so he could call for help, but there wasn't. He remembered seeing one in the kitchen, but the whole downstairs would be under two feet of water by now. He threw off the covers and grabbed the notes he had left on the bedside table. As he reached for his rosary beads, he noticed his hand was trembling and for a brief moment, it seemed strange, almost foreign to him ... as though his hand was someone else's. But he didn't have time for such madness— he had to get out of the house!

He tried to remember if he had left his car keys in his coat pocket like usual, but images of icy waves spilling over the furniture kept breaking his concentration. He couldn't imagine what he was going to see when he rounded the top of the stairs.

But what he saw when he got to the top of the landing terrified him more than even his wildest speculations. He was paralyzed with fear. From the sound of the roaring water, there should have been torrents of water and chunks of ice crashing over the foot of the stairs. But from where he stood, he saw absolutely nothing out of the ordinary.

Everything was calm downstairs. Everything was dry. Yet the thundering rush of waves sounded close enough and strong enough to drown him. His eyesight defied his hearing. Something was very wrong. He stood there, frozen with a singular sense of terror and dread such as he had never experienced before.

Suddenly, before he could even begin to digest what was happening, the roaring sound stopped and the house was silent again. Brother Michael didn't know what to think. He was relieved that the noise had stopped, but he couldn't stop the pounding in his chest. *What had just happened?*

He stood staring down the stairway, knowing he should go and check out the downstairs just to be certain there was no damage. But for the life of him, he didn't want to. Finally, he worked up the nerve and slowly sidled down halfway. Grasping the cherry railing with both hands, he leaned over just enough to peer into the kitchen and family room. Outside, the pristine snow continued to fall, casting a pale sheen over the room. Everything seemed to be in order. Everything was dry. The house was untouched, oblivious to whatever it was that just happened.

Brother Michael couldn't bring himself to go all the way down the stairs. Instead, he crept back up and retreated into his bed. With rosary beads firmly in hand, he pulled the covers up over his chin and tried to pray. But his thoughts were all over the place. He tried to apply his reason to what had just happened. He must have imagined it. Or possibly he had developed some type of hearing disorder. He thought he remembered reading something about a condition that involved hearing noises in your ears. That's what it had to be. But then why did he still feel this sense of intense fear? Was he losing his health, his mind? Or did something evil just happen? And which was more terrifying?

Finally he decided he would try not to worry and promised himself that he would contact the Abbot as soon as he got back to the monastery. The Abbot was not only a wise and prudent soul, he had the gift of discernment, and Brother Michael trusted him implicitly. This calmed him a bit, and he spent the remainder of the night in prayer trying to rid himself of the uneasiness that was sticking to his ribs.

By morning, he was somewhat successful. The snow had stopped, the sun was shining, the driveway was plowed, and the events of the past night seemed more like a bad dream than reality. After a nice strong cup of coffee and a light breakfast, he set out for the second day of the conference. It went very well considering his lack of sleep, and at the end of the day, he gratefully accepted an offer from his friend to bring dinner and a few friends over to the house that evening.

The dinner was delicious, and the company was more of a relief to Brother Michael than he cared to admit. As the evening progressed, so did the conversation. It was a close knit and lively minded group that liked nothing better than a good laugh, and Brother Michael enjoyed the familiar banter between them. It was during one of the rare but comfortable silences that Tim, the son of the owner of the house, turned his attention to Brother Michael.

"And how have you found the house, Brother Michael?"

Brother Michael was surprised by the question, but answered, "Oh, it's very comfortable, thank you. You and your family have been more than generous."

The young man shook his head. "No," he paused. "I mean ... you're welcome, of course. I guess what I meant to say was have you had any feelings at all about the house?"

Brother Michael wasn't sure what to say and he became very conscious of the silence that filled the room. He hadn't mentioned anything of the night before. "Feelings, you say?"

"I mean," Tim continued, "Ever since I was a little boy, I have always felt something strange in this house, something dark. My mother thinks I'm nuts and gets angry with me every time I bring it up. I was wondering if you have felt anything?"

Brother Michael could feel his cheeks blush. He realized how hesitant he was to divulge the events of the night before. The group might very well think he was delusional. "Well, actually, now that you mention it, the strangest thing happened last night..."

At that very instant the lights snapped out, and the entire house went dark except for the small glow of the candle in the center of the table. It was dead quiet, and the soft, flickering candlelight on the startled faces around the table made the rest of the house seem that much darker, almost sinister. Brother Michael felt a cold panic rising into his chest, and for a split second he thought he was going to scream with fright.

"Well well," Tim laughed, and pointing his finger with exaggerated aplomb, said, "and that would be the fuse box. Happens all the time!" He jumped up from his chair, disappeared into the darkness, and, returning with a flashlight, went down to the cellar.

By the time he returned and the electricity was restored, the rest of the group had managed to collect themselves and were already appreciating what a good story it would make. Thankfully, this had a soothing effect on Brother Michael.

"So, Brother Michael," continued Tim jovially, "What was it you were going to say before we were so rudely interrupted?"

The group listened intently as Brother Michael recounted the events of his bizarre first night at the house. When he had finished, there was a collective silence, and an air of seriousness settled upon the gathering.

"I think this calls for a glass of brandy." It was Tim again. He went to the kitchen and returned carrying a tray with six snifters of the amber colored quaff. Brother Michael would normally have declined, but tonight he thought it might do him some good. And it did seem to settle his nerves. He sipped slowly, hoping one of his listeners could come up with a logical, believable explanation. The possibility of a hearing disorder did come up, but no one could remember the name of it. Whatever it was, the group seemed to agree that there was nothing to be done that night, and it was time for all to go home to bed.

As Brother Michael was seeing them to the door, Tim pulled him aside and offered to sleep on the couch in the living room if it would make him feel more comfortable. Brother Michael thanked him for his thoughtfulness but, somewhat hesitantly assured him that he would be fine.

However, not even ten minutes later, when he didn't have the distraction of his companions, the oppressive uneasiness started up again and he regretted not taking Tim up on his offer. In fact he was tempted to run out and see if he might still be in the driveway, but that was silly. He was exhausted by this time but wasn't ready to go upstairs. He attempted to distract himself again by cleaning up the few dishes that were left on the table, but he just couldn't shake it. He tried to convince himself that whatever it was that happened last night was over, but he could still feel that horrible dread. He needed to talk to the Abbot back at the monastery. It was almost one o'clock in the morning, but he knew he wouldn't be able to sleep unless he did something.

He dialed the number and a very sleepy Brother Ambrose picked up the line. Apologizing for the hour, Brother Michael asked to speak to the Abbot. He could hear the curiosity in Brother Ambrose's voice, but he put the call through without any questions. As he waited, Brother Michael looked out the sliding glass doors at the lake. It had started to snow again, and he felt a heaviness in his chest at the very sight of it.

When he heard the click of the call being picked up, he was going to offer another quick apology for the lateness of his call. But before Brother Michael could say a word, he heard the frantic voice of the Abbot in the receiver.

"Brother Michael, oh thank God, Brother Michael!"

The voice on the other line barely even resembled that of the Abbot. Brother Michael's first thought was that something horrible had happened at the monastery, and his mind started racing through all the possibilities.

"I tried to reach you earlier," the Abbot continued. "Get out of that house! I've had a premonition. There is great evil in that house. You are not safe! Get out! GET OUT NOW!"

Brother Michael couldn't speak. He was stunned. And for a moment, paralyzed with fear and confusion.

"But how did you ... where do I go? It's one o'clock in the morn ...?"

"JUST GO! NOW!"

"Y-y-yes father," he stuttered, "I'll leave right away!"

Without another word, Brother Michael hung up the telephone and raced through the house gathering his things. It seemed that he couldn't move fast enough. It was as though the house was boring down on him. He was so frantic and undone that he couldn't believe his body was actually obeying his mind. As he headed for the door, he stopped for a second and tried to remember if he'd left anything upstairs, but quickly decided that even if he did, it was staying there. He flew out the door and ran faster than he had in decades across the snow-covered path to his car.

Once in, he blew a sigh of relief that he had left the keys to the car in his coat pocket. He started it up and sped down the long driveway wondering where he would go once he reached the road. By the grace of God, he remembered the way to an inn located in the village where he had dined several years ago, The Lincklean House.

A young girl with purple hair was sitting at the front desk reading a gossip magazine and chewing gum.

His blustery entrance startled her. "Oh! I'm sorry, sir ... I mean Father. Can I help you?"

Brother Michael couldn't have been happier to see her, purple hair and all. There was something so honest, so simple, and so good about the scene. "Please, yes," he said, realizing he was still out of breath. "Do you have a room available?"

"We certainly do," she chirped, and snapped her gum as she turned to grab a key that was attached to a brass ring.

"Room number twenty-two," she said. "It's very pretty and it's away from the street, so it will be nice and quiet for you."

Brother Michael sighed as he accepted the key from her. "Thank you, miss. It is greatly appreciated, I assure you."

He saw her give him a questioning glance as she slid his credit card through the machine.

"Just sign here and you're all set!" Then, as he scribbled a shaky signature on the receipt, she added, "Are you sure you're okay, Father?"

He looked up at her with an appreciative and reassuring smile. "Yes, young lady. Don't you worry. I'm fine now, and that's all that matters. Thank you so much." He started for the stairs, but turned back to her. "And may the good and merciful God bless you, my angel, ten times over."

Chapter Four

Hide and Seek

Mike's Story

Mike realized he was hungrier than usual when he opened the door and smelled the combination of fresh Paul De Lima coffee and greasy bacon and eggs. And with the almost deafening clamor of china and silverware, he knew he was in exactly the right place to take care of that.

Emma's Cafe was a narrow little hole in the wall with eight marble tables and cherry booths that were covered with more than half a century's worth of initials and memories carved into them. A small linoleum bar complete with stools ran parallel to the booths and separated the cook from the customers. The place only seated fifty people tops, but it was as busy and bustling at seven o'clock in the morning as any New York City nightclub might be at two a.m. Instead of skimpy halter-tops and strappy sandals, however, the fashion trend at Emma's was strictly Carhartts and steel-toed boots.

"Hey Mike!" somebody yelled above the din, "Get your sorry little self down here."

Mike looked down the line of booths and saw his pals seated in their usual spot. Before he even sat down, a pretty blonde came over with a pot of steaming coffee.

"The usual?" she asked without even looking at him.

"Thanks Sherri, but actually ..." Mike grunted as he squeezed himself into the booth. "I'm going for something a little different this morning. I'm going to have two eggs over medium, home fries, crisp bacon, sausage, and a blueberry muffin."

She glanced at Mike, only barely masking her surprise, then without writing anything down, left the booth with a quick, "gotcha."

Bob, a retired history teacher, part-time house painter, and full-time wiseacre looked up from his three-egg omelet. "Whoa. I don't believe *that's* on the diet!" He emptied a container of strawberry jam and spread it lovingly on his toast. "Does the wife know anything about this?"

"No sir, she does not," Mike said like a man throwing caution to the wind. He unfolded his paper napkin and placed it neatly on his lap. "And I'm not afraid of her, either."

His three listeners let out a series of locker-room chuckles.

"Yeah, right," Bob mumbled through his mouthful of toast, "and if I were to march down the street right now and tell Linda what you're about to eat for—breakfast, no less—you don't think you would be shaking in your boots?"

"Not necessarily … well ok, maybe … well yeah, probably. But we won't have to worry about that now, will we? Not if you keep your big mouth shut!"

They all laughed, and Mike shook his head good-heartedly. "You know, I've got to admit. I'm almost fifty years old, and I'm not scared of much. But just one look from that lady, and I'm a Screaming Mimi!"

There was a pause while they all thought this over, then grudgingly nodded their heads in mutual understanding.

Sherri reappeared, deposited Mike's platter in front of him with a clang, refilled everybody's coffee cups, and disappeared again. Mike gave an appreciatory growl and thanked her even though she had already moved on. Cutting into his eggs he said, "Now enough about my diet. What's the news?"

The next half hour was filled with conversation about the who-what-where-when-how-and why of the latest scandals, job referrals, and local politics. Then as usual, by eight thirty, the diner was cleared. The burly flannel-clad contractors had all piled into their separate pick-ups and headed for their job sites. Mike walked out onto the sidewalk, took a deep breath, and rubbed his belly. It was a beautiful April morning. There was a little nip in the air, but the weatherman said it was going to warm up.

After doing some errands around the village, Mike climbed into his truck and was greeted with a big, sloppy kiss from Tessa, the other lady in his life. Her sad brown eyes and soft golden hair never failed to bring a smile. He rubbed her ear playfully.

"Come on, girl," he said as he started up the truck, "Guess it's time to go home and do some work."

Work was the last thing Mike felt like doing. He loved Upstate New York, but the winters seemed to get longer every year. And today, as he drove east toward Nelson, that long-awaited feeling of spring was definitely in the air. The whole countryside seemed to be bursting with fresh, new life, and even though there were still stubborn patches of dirty snow, he could feel the winter cobwebs inside him beginning to thaw. The pale sprays of fresh buds on the maple trees looked like feathery clouds against the sky. He felt that restlessness that always hit him this time of year, that almost overwhelming desire to drop everything and go out and play. "Ahh," he sighed as they got out of his truck, "but a man's got to make a living."

As he and Tessa made their way through the side door, he made a mental list of what he needed to accomplish—call in a few orders, print out some invoices, pay the bills.

"That's not that much," he said to Tessa. "If all goes well, we might have time to toss a ball around."

On hearing the word "ball," Tessa ran back to the door, her feet skidding on the hardwood floors.

Mike laughed. "Not yet, girl. Work first, play later."

Tessa was a three-year-old Terripoo. Mike had bought her for Linda when they moved to their Nelson home three years ago in 1998. It was a good move for Mike. He loved the countryside, the privacy, and, well, everything about it. He worked out of the house, which was great. But his business also required a lot of travel, and Linda got spooked when she was alone in the house at night. And no wonder, it was a huge brown colonial, five thousand square feet, with five fireplaces and loads of windows overlooking the hills.

The previous owner had built the house in 1989, but when you walked into it you would swear it was two hundred years old. He had taken great care right down to the last detail. It even creaked and groaned like an old house. The ceilings were post and beam, the hardware on the doors and cupboards was all black kettle iron. The only room in the house that looked its age was the basement. It had been originally used as a hair salon, but Mike had gutted it and made it into a nice, efficient office for himself. This was where he and Tessa sat; Mike at his computer, and Tessa comfortably stretched out on the Berber carpet.

By this time it was about nine o'clock. Mike was writing out an invoice when he suddenly heard a voice upstairs. It was a little girl's voice, and she was giggling. Tessa heard it too. She raised her head and looked toward the stairway, her ears pointed straight up.

"What the heck?"

His first thought was that it must be Brandy, the little five-year-old girl who lived in the house down the road. Maybe she had wandered. Mike and Linda never locked their doors, and she could easily have slipped inside unnoticed. This didn't sit well with Mike, because they had put a swimming pool in the back yard two years ago. Right from day one, the possibility of a tragedy had loomed over him. Brandy had never done anything like this before, but it was a beautiful spring morning, and days like this one brought out the rascal in everyone.

"Hello?" Mike tried to sound as non-threatening as he could. He didn't want to scare her. But there was no response, just more giggling.

"Who's there? Brandy, is that you?"

He got up from his chair to investigate, but Tessa beat him to it and bounded up the basement stairs ahead of him. As Mike rounded the landing he was surprised to see that Tessa didn't run straight to the side door like she always did. Instead, she turned right and headed for the stairs to the second floor, her tail wagging hysterically.

He couldn't believe it, but was Brandy going upstairs? Just then, he heard the unmistakable sound of little patent-leather shoes running up the hardwood stairs directly above his head, and whoever was wearing them was giggling the whole time.

What the hell?

After he reached the top of the basement stairs he turned immediately and hurried his six-foot, two hundred pound frame as fast he could to the second set of stairs. He must have just missed the little trespasser, but Tessa was rounding the top of the stairs, her whole body wagging, acting as if she were only just inches behind the little girl. Mike could hear the tiny snickers and clicking shoes echo as she ran down the upstairs hallway.

What is that little imp doing? Is she trying to play hide and seek?

"Okay, Brandy ..." he was beginning to get annoyed, but played along anyways. "Peek a boo!" He warbled, "Where are you?"

Mike made it to the top of the stairs just in time to once again catch only Tessa's tail darting around a corner into the one of the spare bedrooms. This little girl was driving him nuts! When he turned into the room, he fully expected to see little Brandy hiding behind the bed with a face full of smiles, and Tessa licking her face.

He was stunned when he saw absolutely no one in the room other than Tessa. It was completely undisturbed. Tessa nosed expectantly under both the twin beds, then looked at Mike—the way she did when Mike would hide her ball in his coat pocket.

This can't be happening, he thought to himself. Brandy was playing with him, she had to be. It was the only explanation. It would have been unusual for sure, but this whole thing was already more than unusual.

"All right," Mike grumbled, "Come on out."

He got down on his knees and looked under the beds. There was nothing but a couple of dust balls. Tessa followed him to the closet, and again there was nothing. This was really starting to freak him out. There was definitely someone in this house. Who was it, and where the hell did they go?

Just then, the thought occurred to Mike that maybe it wasn't just a little girl being playful on a beautiful spring morning. Maybe it was really an intruder who broke in to steal something, and whoever it was, they were still in the house. They had to be.

He could feel his adrenaline kick into high gear, and he looked around the room for something he could use as a weapon. There wasn't anything but a heavy brass lamp. He unplugged it, picked it up, and removed the shade.

Slowly, purposefully, he crept through the entire upstairs with lamp in hand. He became more and more worried as he looked under every bed, opened every closet, and checked every nook and cranny that could possibly hide a person. Then he started to think of Linda. She would go ballistic if she knew about this. He had to get to the bottom of this now, or she would never feel safe in this house again. He checked every inch of the upstairs again, then went back downstairs and gave it the same treatment. But the house was as still and silent as a Sunday morning. The only conclusion that Mike could come up with was that whomever it was that snuck into his house must have somehow snuck right past him again without him noticing.

Back down in his office, Mike tried to get some work done in the afternoon, but his efforts were fruitless. His mind kept trying to make sense of the morning's events. He felt like a mouse in a maze. He kept going back to the beginning, but every turn he made, he hit a wall. Nothing added up.

Who was *that in my house? How long had they been there before Tessa and I heard them? How did they get out again without me seeing them?*

Mike would have thought that he had lost his mind except for the fact that Tessa had obviously heard it too. The idea briefly fluttered through his mind that it was something supernatural, but Mike couldn't even begin to go down that path. He had never even entertained the notion.

Worst of all, what was he going to say to Linda? They had been together since they were kids, and she knew him better than anyone. If she found out about this, she would never sleep in the house again. It was that simple.

At around four in the afternoon, Mike gave up on his work and climbed the basement stairs again. He scoured the whole house one more time. Linda would be home around five. He wasn't sure what he wanted to find, just something that would make sense, something he could tell her. But there was nothing—not even the smallest trace—that could account for the morning's mystery.

His heart started to race as the minutes drew closer. He decided that if he didn't find some sort explanation, he wasn't going to tell her a thing. And that was risky. He had never kept anything from Linda before; he'd never been able to. She was too sharp. After twenty-eight years of marriage, she would know something was up.

Mike finally sat down and took a long, deep breath. He had to compose himself. This was going to be the performance of a lifetime. It had to be. He had to be as cool, as charming, and as cunning as a crooked politician.

When she breezed through the doorway with a couple of grocery bags stuffed in her arms, he forced himself to pause so as not to grab them too enthusiastically. What Mike needed to be was neither too helpful, nor too aloof—not too quiet, nor overly talkative. He needed to be *exactly* like he always was every other blasted day of his life, and that was going to be the hardest thing he'd ever done.

But somehow he managed to pull it off. He was the perfect picture of an ordinary man, who'd had an ordinary day at work, and was looking forward to spending an ordinary evening with his wife.

And so it went for weeks. He never mentioned anything to Linda, nor to anyone else for that matter—certainly not his pals at Emma's. He and Tessa drove into town every weekday morning just like they always did, had breakfast, and then came back to work.

But Mike was anything but his normal self. His mind kept going back to the maze, and every time it did he would hit the wall again. A tiny little bolt in his thinking process—one that he'd forgotten even existed—had fallen out of place, and Mike was left hanging all alone in a strange and thoroughly uncomfortable space.

Eventually though, time performed its magic, and as spring made its graceful exit, so did the thoughts of that morning. The trees were rich with leaves now, and the sky was endless. The rolling hills around Mike's house overlapped and intertwined, creating a lush tapestry in shades of green and blue. The gardens were in full bloom, the pool was and up and running, and the house smelled of honeysuckle and mint.

And it was softball season. As always during this time of year, Mike and Linda were standing down at the park watching their oldest son's game. It was a warm evening, and there was a slight breeze coming off the lake. Softball season was always fun because it was a time for the spectators, as well as the players, to catch up with friends they might not have seen since the summer before.

Sometime during the third inning, Mike was standing just about two yards ahead of Linda and one of her girlfriends. They were chatting away like two little sparrows about things that only women are interested in. Mike was watching the game. Just then, Amelia—a former classmate and one of those people he hadn't seen since last season—came up to say hello. They exchanged pleasantries, then out of the clear blue sky, she asked, "Have you seen the child ghost yet?"

Mike felt like he'd been hit in the back of his head with a two by four. It must have shown, because Linda spoke from behind him with a combination of curiosity and concern in her voice. "What is it, Mike?"

God, she notices everything! He thought to himself, and his heart started to race. He shot Amelia a quick glance that screamed, *stop now!* Then with as innocent an expression as he could muster, he turned back to Linda. "What?"

It worked—at least momentarily. Linda resumed conversation with her friend, and Mike turned back to Amelia. He looked her square in the eyes. "Later," he mouthed.

Amelia looked totally perplexed. But why wouldn't she? She didn't understand that if Linda thought for one minute there was a ghost in the house... but she didn't really know her that well. But thank God, Amelia took the hint and moseyed over to another group. Mike turned back toward the field, folded his arms, and tried to focus on the game. But wham! He found himself right back in the damned maze again.

Ghost child...? Ghost? What the hell is she talking about? There's no such thing as ghosts! And even if there were, there's no way that the little girl who ran through the house that day was a...!

If Linda even heard that word, it would send her through the roof! This was bad. He looked over and saw Amelia standing by the concession stand. He needed to talk with her.

"Honey," he turned to Linda. "I'm going to get some coffee. Do you want some?"

Linda looked up and shook her head. "No thanks."

Mike walked over to Amelia and he thought she looked a little apprehensive when she saw him approach. "So what was that all about, Mike?" she asked.

"Oh, Jesus," Mike replied, shaking his head. "If Linda thought for even a second that there was a ghost in our house, we would have to move out. Not kidding. I know it sounds crazy, but ... well, never mind. Now, what's this about a *child ghost*?"

Amelia crinkled her face and looked over at Linda. "Really..." she said more like a statement than a question, then turned back to Mike. She went on to explain that she used to get her hair cut in Mike's basement when it was the salon. She remembered the owner frequently mentioned seeing the ghost of a little girl, usually standing in the five-foot fireplace in the family room. "I guess she was around four years old... perfectly friendly and everything. I mean, nothing to be afraid of."

Yeah right, Mike thought to himself, *nothing to be afraid of.* His mind was reeling. *It can't be. I can't be hearing this.* But it was really the only thing that made any sense at all, the only path in the maze where he didn't slam into the wall. "Do me a favor, Amelia. Don't ever mention this to Linda."

She smiled a little suspiciously, and turned back to her friends. Mike went to get the coffee feeling like his world, the one he thought he could understand and work with, had just slipped through his fingers like a handful of Jell-O. As he walked back with a steaming cup of coffee in his hand, he looked over at Linda. She had her arms folded together neatly, comfortably chatting away but keeping her eyes on the field. She looked so innocent and naïve. *If this is true, I'm going to have to sell the house.*

But he didn't. Instead, Mike spent the next few days and weeks walking on pins and needles, listening, and waiting for any sign of his little intruder, his little … ghost. He hadn't seen or heard anything in months and all he could do was hope that it stayed that way.

And thank heavens, his little ghost must not have been in the mood to play. Weeks turned into months. The seasons of Mike and Linda's lives continued on with no ghostly interruptions, and the twists and turns of daily life managed to render the events of that morning to be like that of a dream.

It was another spring morning two years later. Mike had gone to Emma's for his morning dose of breakfast and banter, then he and Tessa made their way home. Tessa was relaxing, and Mike was doing some work just like before, though they were now in the new office he'd built on the second floor of the garage.

It was a little chilly outside, but the sun was shining through the windows, and Mike was looking forward to getting some work done. They had gone for a walk after breakfast, and Tessa was zonked in a sunspot on the carpet. Mike was listening to her low, steady breathing when he heard it—the soft, playful laughter of a little girl!

It's her!

But he wasn't even in the same building! She couldn't have followed him to his new office. Ghosts don't follow people! He couldn't believe his ears, but it was unmistakable. He could hear her little shoes running up the stairs toward the closed office door at the top. It was the same little girl, and he knew it! And this time, by God, he was going to catch her!

Mike and Tessa leapt toward the door at exactly the same time. Mike got there first and flung it open. "Okay you little …? Where *are* you?"

But as before, there was nothing.

Mike and Tessa stood staring at the empty stairwell for several seconds before Mike heard a final, tortuously sassy giggle right in front of his face … and then she was gone.

The two of them must have stood there for five minutes. Mike wasn't sure what he was feeling. Of course he was absolutely flabbergasted, just as he'd been before. But this time it was different. Now that he knew what he was dealing with—and he couldn't believe he was even thinking that— there was an element of friendship, playfulness, even reunion.

Finally he just turned to Tessa, "Oh well, old girl, I guess there's not a damned thing we can do about it." Tessa gave a wag of her tail and went back to her sunspot. Mike shook his head then returned to his desk and got back to work.

When Linda came home that afternoon, Mike didn't tell her what had happened. Once again, he couldn't. But it was easier this time. A certain acceptance had set it. It was almost as if he understood that the little girl wouldn't bother Linda. It was only Tessa and Mike that she wanted to play with.

It wasn't until a year and a half later, when they had sold the house and moved to Pennsylvania, that he finally told Linda about his little ghost. He couldn't believe he'd been able to wait that long and even less that he'd been able to carry it off.

"I don't know what it was that I saw or heard those mornings. I won't say it was a ghost, but I know for a fact it wasn't human. And believe me, I know it doesn't make a lick of sense."

Her big blue eyes grew as wide as saucers as she listened to his story and took it all in. She was sweet, very respectful of the intensity of his experience, and he could tell that she never once doubted his sanity.

Mike told her everything from beginning to end and when he was finally through, he took a long, deep breath and blew the weight of the last three years off his shoulders.

"Oh my God, Mike!" Linda said. "I knew it! I knew there was something in that house. I never saw or heard her, but I felt it, believe me. And the whole time I thought I'd lost my mind!"

Mike watched her face as she connected all the dots. She was silent for several minutes, then looked up at him with just a hint of reproach. "You mean that whole time you knew and you didn't …"

Uh oh, Mike thought, *here it comes.*

"Oh, well..." she eventually sighed. "I guess it's a good thing you didn't tell me." She stood up, gave Tessa a pat on the head and looked back at Mike. "Because we definitely would have had to sell the house."

Chapter Five

The Midnight Gardener

Eve's Story

"Yup! We have cake mix, but no frosting … you do? Is it chocolate?"

Fifteen-year-old Eve rifled through her mom's kitchen cupboards with both hands, the portable phone balanced between her jaw and her left shoulder. Winnie, a big old sweetheart of a dog with a scruffy coat of hair and eyes that could melt Alaska stood watching, her expression a hilarious combination of curiosity and unflinching devotion. With her head cocked to one side and her ears straight out, her eyes followed Eve to the refrigerator.

"Uh oh," Eve said into the phone as she scanned the inside, "We don't have any eggs. You do? Ok, good. I'll be over in two minutes. I'm leaving right now. I'll cut through the back yard." She slammed the refrigerator door and, still balancing the phone on her left shoulder, started to gather her things. "Oh wait, and Lindy …" she blurted breathlessly, "there was a message from Aunt Kathie on the machine this afternoon. Can't believe it, but things are looking up for tonight! I'll tell you about it when I get there!" She pushed the end button on the cordless phone, tossed it onto the laundry pile that she was supposed to have folded, rolled her huge blue eyes, then picked it up again She dialed Lindy's number. "Wait. Sorry. Did you say you *do* have the frosting?"

Seven minutes later, Eve popped down the gravel driveway toward the garage. Her long blonde ponytail bounced cheerfully from side to side, while the untied laces of her sneakers snapped back and forth in unison. Her mother was away for the weekend, and her Aunt Kathie was staying at the house "to keep an eye on things."

One of the "things," of course, was Eve. Consequently, the girls had settled on a nice, wholesome evening that included Lindy's hot tub, a cake, and a movie. *Of course*, Eve thought with a devious smile as she remembered Aunt Kathie's message on the answering machine, *plans could change considerably.*

Once she reached the garage, she squeezed herself in between the side of the building and the split rail fence that bordered the lawn. It was getting dark, and she had to block her face from the twigs and bramble. But once she made it past the garage, there would be a well-worn path through the woods that she and Lindy had formed over the years. It wasn't a big stretch of woods, only about thirty yards or so. Truth was, she could walk it blindfolded if she had to. Then all she had to do was climb over the fence and she'd come out in the corner of Lindy's backyard.

If she hadn't been so delightfully absorbed in her mischievous musings, Eve would have noticed what a beautiful September night it was. With her keen sense of design, she would have loved how the leaves cast a mosaic of pale moon shadows all around her. She would have appreciated the elegance of a single yellow leaf that curled silently down to her feet. That certain smell in the air would have signaled to her the end of another summer and the approach of a new school year. At the very least, as she came upon the darkest, most isolated part of the path, she would have seen the completely incongruous figure of a man that stood beneath the boughs of honeysuckle blocking her path.

But she didn't see him at all. Not until she almost ran right into him. The first thing she noticed was the rusted pruning shears in the bib pocket of his overalls. She looked up and saw his eyes staring directly into hers, and in that split second, all thoughts of teenage tyranny were extinguished. Her brain, her breath, her heart, everything it seemed but her stomach, slammed into reverse.

Then, as happens in situations like these, Eve's mind plunged forward, working at ridiculous speeds; taking in images, seeking possible explanations, and assessing the degree of danger. She saw that he was an older man with a messy crop of white hair above his pale, creased forehead. He almost looked like her grandfather, and her first instinct was to apologize for practically running him over. But then she realized that it was unusual for *anyone* to be walking on this path, let alone an old man in overalls.

There was something so different about him. He didn't respond in a normal way. He didn't appear startled or worried at all, even though she could easily have knocked him down. He just looked at her, acknowledging her presence. But his face was unresponsive, like that of a person walking on a crowded city sidewalk. It was almost as if he was familiar with this path, had come upon her a thousand times before, and was simply waiting for her to pass so he could be on his way.

His eyes were a pale, pale blue, almost gray, and actually quite gentle looking. He must have been tall and muscular in his youth, but age had left him bent and frail. The baggy overalls that looked as old as he did hung loosely from his still broad shoulders. He looked tired and weary, as if he was heading home from a long day in the garden. But there was something about him; something Eve couldn't put a name to that was very, very sad.

Eve then felt the strangest and most unexpected question crawling its way up the base of her spine … *is he even real?* She had never had the occasion to ask herself such a question, and the terrifying absurdity of it caught her so off guard that she instinctively turned around and bolted for home. Like a young filly, her legs stretched their entire length, while the sounds of panic pounded in her ears. When she made it back to her garage and had to maneuver her body between it and the fence, she glanced back and was stunned to find that he was nowhere to be seen. It was only a matter of seconds, she thought to herself. There was no way a man of his age could have disappeared that quickly. She looked again, but the path and greenery around it were silent and still, almost stubbornly so, admitting nothing of her encounter only moments before.

Poor Winnie was already in doggie dreamland when Eve came crashing through the back door. She jumped up before she had regained her equilibrium and knocked her rump against the table, which wobbled just enough to tip over the lamp, which landed right next to Louise the cat, who had also been enjoying a nap on the couch. The noise and confusion of the cat's exit were considerable. It sent Winnie back to her bed with her nose to the floor and her tail tightly secured between her legs. But Eve didn't notice. She was too busy trying to keep herself in one piece.

Lindy! She had to call Lindy! Eve ran over to the counter to grab the phone, but it wasn't in the charger. *Dammit! Where was the phone?* She thought of the millions of times her mother had scolded her for not putting it back into the jack. *Dammit!* She needed to find the phone. Frustration and nerves were quickly gaining the edge on her, and she felt like she was going to scream when she finally heard it ring.

Following the muffled sound, she found the phone right where she had left it—on top of the laundry pile. It was Lindy.

What followed sounded more like a flock of geese landing in a pond than a single, teenage girl. Winnie flattened herself on her bed as much as she could in an effort to become invisible.

"So there's no way I'm walking over there now," Eve concluded with a final squawk. "Not unless you come and get me. Okay. Wait! No. Wait! Don't take the trail. Take the sidewalk. Okay. Bye."

Eve hurried around to the front window, pulled the sheer curtain aside, and waited for Lindy to appear. It was dark now, but an old lantern that someone had long ago wired right into the trunk of a maple tree cast a dim yellow glow on the sidewalk. A small spattering of golden leaves, the first victims of autumn, had fallen on the dark green lawn.

It seemed like it was taking Lindy forever. And for some reason, with each passing second, Eve became more and more aware of the silence in the house. She had spent many evenings alone without batting an eye, but this was different. The silence was stunning. It was almost as if the house itself was holding its breath, waiting, watching. Was it because there was someone in the house? If she turned around right now, would there be someone standing right behind her ... some *thing* standing right behind her?

Eve didn't know what to do, where to run. She was beginning to feel like a can of spilled paint when she finally saw Lindy rounding the corner. She'd never been more relieved to see anyone in her life. Like a streak of lightning she was out the front door, across the lawn, and grabbing at Lindy's arms for dear life.

"Oh my God, Eve," Lindy said, "What happened?"

Anything Eve managed to blurt out was for the most part unintelligible until they had reached Lindy's house, locked the doors, and were safely inside her bedroom.

"I swear," Eve panted. "He was a ghost."

"Well what did he look like? I mean did he look all cloudy like you could see through him?"

"No!" Eve answered as if she had been waiting for Lindy to ask. "That's the thing. He didn't look anything like you see in the movies. He looked just like you. Like I could have reached out and touched him." Eve closed her eyes and shuddered as she tried to shake off the thought of it. "But I know if I did, there wouldn't have been anything to touch! He was so real ... but he wasn't."

"Wow," was all Lindy could say. But that was enough. She always had a way of calming Eve down. It was just her nature. And she was also the more practical of the two.

"You forgot the cake mix," she said with a smile as she rubbed Eve's shoulder briskly with the purpose of bringing her back to the task at hand.

Eve's eyes widened. "Whoops! And I forgot my bathing suit, too."

"Don't worry. We have extra bathing suits around here. And we can go back to your house and get the cake mix."

"No way," said Eve.

"Okay, then we can walk to the store and buy another one."

"No way."

"Yes way," Lindy coaxed. "We'll be fine. The ghost is on the other side of the street. Plus, ghosts only come around when a you're alone."

"Well … okay," Eve acquiesced. "But let's make it quick."

So the two girls headed back into the night trying to act as if nothing had happened, though truth be told, they were a bit less chatty than usual. After they had secured the cake mix and were on their way back to Lindy's house, Lindy stopped in her tracks.

"Oh yeah, Eve, what was the message you got that you were so excited to tell me about?"

"Oh my God!" Eve rolled her eyes and slapped her forehead with the palm of her hand. "I can't believe I forgot! When I got home this afternoon, there was a message from Aunt Kathy, and she said that she would be home between 8:00 and 8:30!"

She turned and looked at Lindy with a conspiratorial eye but was surprised to find a look of complete bewilderment on her face.

"I don't get it," Lindy said.

Eve rolled her eyes in frustration. "Duh, that means that she's only going to be there for half an hour tonight! And *that* means…" a devilish smile made its way across her lips, "that we could have some friends over to my house and do whatever we want!"

It took Lindy several seconds to figure out how Eve had gone from point A to point B, but of all the people in the world, Lindy understood Eve's mind better than anyone else. She looked at Eve with humorous affection.

"Eve," she said deliberately, "I don't think Aunt Kathie meant that she was *only* going to be at your house between 8:00 and 8:30. I think she meant that she would *arrive* at your house between 8:00 and 8:30."

Deep furrows appeared between Eve's eyebrows as she mulled this over. "Oooohh … darn," she said. Then after a moment or two, she added with a smile, "Well, I guess that means we really are just going to have cake, hot tub, and movie."

And that's just what they did.

***

Eve never took the shortcut to Lindy's house again, and the old man on the path politely withdrew back into the shadows of her memory. As the seasons passed, he became something she only thought of now and then. That is until one snowy Sunday afternoon over a year and a half later.

The girls and a group of their friends had enjoyed a full day of sledding and were now sprawled around Lindy's coffee table, filling their stomachs and warming their bones. Their scarlet cheeks and the flames from the fireplace seemed to be the only color in the room as the thickening snow and approaching dusk robbed the day of its light.

As inevitably happens when you get a group of teenage girls together in a darkening room, the conversation turned to ghosts. They oohed and ahhed while each of them recounted their most titillating tales.

"Hey Eve!" Lindy cut in, "Do you remember the one you saw out back?"

All eyes turned to Eve as she described her run-in with the old gardener on the path. She was the only one of the group that had actually *seen* a ghost, so of course they asked her to explain exactly what he looked like. As she described him, Eve's eyes turned inward, back to that night on the path, and she felt that peculiar sadness that she had felt so long ago. She told them of his white hair, his sad eyes, and the overalls with the pruning shears tucked in the bib. She remembered every detail, and it actually felt good to talk of him again.

"Oh my God, that's Mr. Hartell!"

It was Lindy's mother who spoke. She had remained unnoticed by the girls until now, and they all turned to look at her. "You just described him exactly."

She paused for a long moment, and then continued, "He was a very gentle soul who loved nothing better than to be in his vegetable garden. He lived right over there." She pointed toward a small contemporary house out back that was two doors up from Eve's and shook her head. "Such a sad thing."

A seldom-heard silence lingered in the room as the group of girls digested the new information. Eve wasn't sure how she felt. She certainly felt less crazy and she supposed it was nice that she could finally put a name to her ghost. She was going to ask Lindy's mother how he died, but for some reason she felt she already knew the answer.

And that sadness seemed closer, more tangible than ever.

Chapter Six

The Bonnie Brae Loch

Mary's Story

It was in the wee hours of the morning that Mary was summoned out of an unusually deep sleep by an equally unusual sound. It was a sporadic, high-pitched chirping sound, almost exactly like that of a cardinal, but it couldn't have been a cardinal because it was coming from inside the house. At first it fit into her dream, but it stubbornly continued until it wound its way into her consciousness and finally woke her up. She hadn't had a good night's sleep since she could remember and, if it were at all possible, she would have ignored it. But the sound persisted.

With an inner groan, Mary begrudgingly opened one eye. Had one of the cats caught a bird and managed to bring it in the house? Images of a bird flailing about her bedroom trying to escape the uncompromising claws of her three cats came crowding into her head. It had happened before and it wasn't her favorite way to start a day, and right now she wasn't sure she was too fond of the felis silvestris catus anymore. She squeezed her eyes and braced herself for another gruesome rescue. Then she remembered. It couldn't be the cats. She had gotten them all inside last night. Then what on earth could that noise be?

Mary wasn't afraid at all. She knew there would be a practical explanation and probably a very easy solution. What frustrated her was that somehow it was going to involve her getting out of bed, and she wanted to avoid that at all cost. She didn't even want to move a muscle because then she would never be able to get back to sleep. If only she could just figure out what it was and conclude that it wasn't dangerous in any way, she felt sure she could ignore it altogether.

Then it came to her. *The smoke detector! That's it!* The battery was dying, and as usual it chose the least opportune time to begin its death rattle. She would take it out and replace it in the morning. For now a couple of pillows would work nicely. Quite pleased with herself, Mary piled two soft pillows over her head, and floated back into the lavender shadows.

The following day was an unusually warm one for November and probably the last of the year, so Mary took the day off from work to put her perennial garden to bed and do the final outdoor preparations for the winter. The physical work felt good but as always, it took longer than she'd anticipated, and by four thirty in the afternoon Mary was dead tired. As she emptied the last wheelbarrow into the compost, she was relieved that she had made plans for the evening—a little company, and the reprieve from cooking was always a welcome one.

After a piping-hot shower, Mary put on a change of clothes and walked over to her bedroom window to check out the garden. Combing out her hair, she looked down at the weed-free soil and neatly trimmed clumps and was pleased with her day's work. She took in a long, self-satisfied breath and looked up at the sky. A cold front was coming in from the Southwest. Huge, dense clouds rose from the darkening twilight like medieval dragons, their long forked tongues stretching horizontally across the sky. A full moon skirted in and out as the clouds moved swiftly to the North. It looked more like the set of *The Hound of the Baskervilles* than the village of Cazenovia.

"Wow," Mary said to her cats who were all eyeing her from their separate perches, "Spooooooooky."

Evidently, not only the cats, but everyone else thought so too. Because an hour later, when she met up with her friends at their favorite haunt, each one of them commented on how remarkable the clouds had been, and the mood had been set for some lighthearted skullduggery.

And the Brae Loch Inn was the perfect setting for it. Standing on the corner of Route 20 and East Lake Rd., it was a popular place for locals as well as tourists. Its Scottish heritage accounted for the dark, cozy atmosphere of the tavern, making it a favorite hideaway on a cold winter's evening. The downstairs included three cozy dining areas, each with its own gas fireplace to accommodate even the weariest of travelers. The pine walls were made invisible by framed photographs of famous guests and Scottish prints. Backlit stained glass windows offered more ambiance than light, but antique lamps that were tastefully scattered about produced a warm glow. Just to the left of the hostess desk was the parlor, an inviting room with a fireplace all its own and decorated with a masculine formality in mind. At the far end of the room stood a pool table surrounded by Victorian velvets and marble, lending a visitor to feel that they had somehow slipped into to a different era, where men retired to the parlor after dinner for a scotch, a smoke, and a game of billiards.

It was in the parlor that Mary and her friends retreated for a friendly game of pool. It was a comfortable gathering where the conversation flowed as easily as the cabernet, and before long, the subject turned to ghosts.

"Actually," Mary leaned over the pool table to take aim, "The Brae Loch is supposed to have a ghost or two!" And with that, she hit the cue ball with a little more pop than usual and sunk her shot.

"No kidding?" replied Patrick keeping his eyes on the table.

Mary and Patrick had been friends for several years, and she knew that her statement would rouse his curiosity. He considered himself clairvoyant. She considered him a bit of a know-it-all when it came to certain things. In any case, she knew it would ruffle his telepathic feathers to hear of a ghost right under his nose that he must have overlooked. She was thoroughly enjoying her advantage.

"Oh yeah," she goaded him as she took her second shot. She missed, but the game was far from over. "They're all over the place. One on the stairs, one in the front room, and a nasty little son of a gun in the back room."

"Really." Patrick's eyes narrowed just a bit as he set up his shot. Mary recognized the look. He had gone for the bait.

"Yup!" Mary nodded. "I've never seen a thing, but almost every employee here has seen one ghost or another. No one will close up at night alone except for PJ, and even he gets spooked."

Patrick didn't respond, just smiled and took his shot. He hit the intended target and sunk the nine, but Patrick groaned as the cue ball spiraled backwards and sent the eight ball into the corner pocket. Mary made a halfhearted attempt to not gloat, and fortunately for Patrick's ego, no one else was paying much attention. A vicious competition had developed over at the dartboard.

About a half hour later PJ the bartender, a thoroughly likable young man dressed in a dark plaid vest and white shirt, rose from the shadows like the butler in an old movie. "I'm taking off, guys. The place is empty except for you. Let me know if you want anything else before I close up."

Everyone declined, and Mary was getting her coat when Patrick asked her if she would like to stay for another game of pool. She playfully wondered if this was about his last shot or the ghosts.

"Sure, why not?" She said and hung her coat back on the coat rack.

After they said goodnight to their friends, they went and found PJ wandering around the kitchen shutting the lights off and locking doors.

"So you're going to stick around?"

"Guess so," Mary said, "I'll have another Cabernet."

"And a Magic Hat for me," added Patrick.

"Will do," replied PJ. "I'll be just a couple of minutes."

When he delivered the drinks, PJ had included a third glass with just an inch of water in it. He neatly placed the two drinks on the table. Then, as he lowered the glass of water, he said with the tone of a conspirator, "Now you do remember, don't you, that it has just become illegal to smoke in any public place in New York State?"

"Yes we do," they responded in unison and with knowing smiles.

"That's good," PJ said without acknowledging the smiles. "Don't forget to shut the lights out." He wandered over and turned off the gas fireplace and locked the back door. "Goodnight," he said with a smile before disappearing into the darkness.

Mary and Patrick each immediately lit up a cigarette and headed for the pool table. "Ah," Mary gave a contented sigh. "There's nothing I like better than having a smoke, a glass of wine, and playing pool ... all at the same time."

"I agree!" Patrick laughed. "But lets skip the pool. How about we go check out those Brae Loch ghosts you were talking about?"

Mary smiled affectionately. "Funny, I had a feeling you were going to say that."

They put their pool cues away, extinguished their cigarettes in the extra glass of water, shut off the lights in the parlor, and headed out to the main dining area. "Okay," Mary said, "Supposedly there is one ghost over here."

The room was dark, but their way was made easier by the exit light above the door. They walked directly to their left, where four booths were tucked against the wall opposite from the fireplace. She pointed toward the fireplace.

"I don't know too much about it, but a couple of the waitresses say they have seen a little girl over there."

Patrick nodded and stood quietly.

"Feel anything?" Mary asked after a bit. Although she was definitely having fun, there was an element of disappointment when Patrick shook his head.

"Nope. Where's the second ghost?"

Mary led him over near the bar and, with an exaggerated wave of her hand, presented the staircase. "I guess a couple of people have seen a male figure here on the stairs, usually heading up as if returning to his room."

Patrick stopped again for a moment and looked dejected. "Nope. Don't feel a thing. Maybe it's the beer—dulls the senses.'

"Probably," Mary chuckled, then made her way across the middle dining area toward the very back of the building, where two broad slate steps led to a sunken dining area. This small, L-shaped room was the least used dining room at the Inn. Probably because it was so far away from the friendly hustle and bustle of the rest of the rooms.

With every step they took, it grew darker and darker, further and further away from the last emergency light. Although Mary wasn't at all afraid, she had never been back this far when the lights were off, and the darkness and loneliness of the room didn't go unnoticed. She carefully walked down the steps holding the railing as she went. "I guess it's back here, somewhere in this corner. I guess one of the cleaning crew was mopping the floor back here late one night and something scared him so much that he threw the mop on the floor, ran out, and never stepped foot in the building again." Then, on a humorous note, she added, "Apparently, this oversized puff of smoke has some serious issues with his ego."

"Really." Patrick said, and he wandered about the small room. "Sometimes, in order to feel anything, I have to kind of zone out and focus."

While Mary waited for Patrick to zone out, she looked about the room straining to see in the darkness. She saw a fireplace that had been sealed over with cement and was surprised that she had never noticed that before. *Humph*, she thought to herself, *that's odd*. Then she turned around and watched Patrick, waiting for some sort of reaction. He started back up the slate steps, and Mary figured it was another wash, and it was time to go home.

She was just about to join him when, as swiftly and as deadly as the blade of a guillotine, she felt the space behind her disappear. It was as though some unfathomable force had sucked the air out and left a whirling, bottomless vacuum that threatened to suck her in.

"Damn!"

It was all she could manage to say. Her legs and arms wouldn't move, couldn't move. She was afraid that if she even tried to move, she would be sucked into the consuming force behind her. She instinctively knew that even if she could somehow manage to turn around, whatever it was she would see would be unbearable, huge, and overwhelmingly masculine, but not a man. *At least, not a man anymore!*

It was horrible. It was powerful. And it was malevolent. And it was *right behind* her breathing down her neck. She looked up at Patrick and saw the whites of his eyes reflecting the very shock and terror that was about to swallow her in one gulp.

"Oh God," she croaked, but it was barely audible. She felt so small, so helpless, and so ridiculously incapable of moving. She could feel this maniacal force bearing down on her, hovering above, behind her, challenging her to turn around and look. It was as if he was laughing at her, mocking and taunting her with all the fury and rage of a wounded animal.

She could hear Patrick saying, "Come on, let's get out of here," but she couldn't move. Every part of her mind, body, and soul was reeling, but she was trapped, pinned to where she stood by this impossible, invisible energy.

You think you're so smart, don't you? You are nothing compared to me!

She didn't hear it with her ears, but it reverberated through her like an electric shock and she remembered her flippant comment earlier about the ghost having some issues.

What was happening? She saw Patrick come across the room toward her, his jaw set, his eyes dark with determination, and his hands reaching for her. Thank God! He knew what was going on and he was going to help her. Mary was hopeful, but at the same time she was terrified that if Patrick even touched her, something horrible would happen, something even worse. As he approached, a blinding terror gripped her by the throat.

"That's it!" Patrick said gruffly, and he grabbed her forcibly by the hand. "Let's go!"

He pulled Mary toward himself and, without a second's pause, placed his body between her and the … the whatever it was, and hurried her back up the slate steps to the middle dining room.

As soon as she felt she was out of reach, Mary broke away from Patrick and ran through the maze of dining rooms. She ran as though she were running for her life. She didn't stop, didn't even look back, and was later embarrassed to admit that she didn't even think of Patrick. It wasn't until she was in the parking lot outside the building that she stopped to try and catch her breath.

"Holy Jesus!" Patrick had his hands on Mary's shoulders. "What the hell was that?"

Mary was panic stricken, her eyes wild with fear. "Patrick let's go! He's following us!" She turned to run. Patrick grabbed her again.

"Hold it, Mary! Calm down! He's not following you. *He can't go anywhere.*"

Mary looked at him. *Oh God,* she thought, *Patrick doesn't understand!* She wanted to explain, but she couldn't catch her breath. She couldn't form the words, and there wasn't time.

"He's following us!" It was all she could say. She broke free and started to run, but where could she run? She couldn't go home, he would follow her there. She felt like a cowering, trapped animal. Her nerves seemed to be spilling all over the pavement. She turned back and saw Patrick following after her. She could see he was alarmed. She didn't know what to do. She wanted to stop, to calm down, but she was insane with fear. What was happening?

Patrick caught up to her and took her firmly by the shoulders and looked her square in the face. "Listen," he yelled, "that guy in there is a ghost! *He can't go anywhere!* That's why he's such a miserable son of a bitch!"

Mary looked at him, trying to take in his words. After several moments, she felt the first bit of hope. "Are you sure, Patrick?"

"I'm positive. He's been stuck in that room for who knows how long. He just decided to scare the pants off you tonight, and he was successful. But don't let him get the better of you Mary. You've got to calm down."

Mary felt tears well up in her eyes. "Damn him! Damn him!"

"Somebody already did, but go ahead and damn him. Now, let's get you home."

Mary allowed him to walk her home. Yet with every step, a battle was being waged in her mind between the logic of what Patrick was saying and the inner certainty that whatever it was, it was following her. Waves of panic would swell up inside her and stop her dead in her tracks.

"You're absolutely sure, Patrick?"

"Absolutely. Keep moving."

After a lot of stopping and starting, they finally made it to Mary's house. It was early yet, and although Mary felt exhausted, the last thing she would be able to do was sleep. They lit a fire and sat on the couch. Patrick wrapped his arms around her and promised not to leave until Mary felt sure that she hadn't been followed. She curled her legs up and snuggled in. It felt good. She started to feel safe again.

"I thought you were right behind me," Patrick said. "I was going up the stairs and all of a sudden I felt something... something so strong that it almost knocked me over. At that exact moment, I heard you say *damn!* I looked over at you and saw this huge dark shadow *right behind you!*"

Mary cringed at the thought and wiggled closer into Patrick's arms. "Are you *absolutely sure* that a ghost can't follow someone?"

"Absolutely," said Patrick. "And I promise I won't leave until you are as sure as I am."

The two of them sat in silence, staring at the warm glow of the fireplace. Mary was trying to gather the pieces of herself, almost as if she were cleaning up after a storm. One of her cats jumped up on the couch and curled himself up in the crook of her knees, his throaty purr vibrating against her thighs. Patrick gave her a little squeeze, and Mary thanked him with a comfortable sigh. She was starting to feel more like herself. She was beginning to feel safe again. And after a time, her limbs begin to relax and she could feel the sweet softness of sleep spread slowly through her body

"Patrick?" she whispered.

"Yeah?"

Her words were barely audible. "I never want to see another ghost again as long as I live."

Patrick nodded, and after several minutes felt Mary's body finally relax into the steady, even breathing of sleep.

Somewhere, in early hours of the morning, Mary was awakened by a piercingly loud sound. *Chirp! Chirp!* She could feel Patrick's body twitch.

"What the hell …?" He said, his voice groggy with sleep.

Without opening her eyes, Mary smiled to herself. "Oh don't worry, Patrick" she mumbled, "That's just the smoke detector. I guess I forgot to change the batteries."

Chapter Seven

Winter Storm

Danny's Story

Ever since he found his first arrowhead as a boy, Danny Weiskotten developed an intense curiosity about local history. The soil, the rocks, and even the trees of Cazenovia were, in his young mind, filled with treasures and clues to the lives of generations long past. Now as a man in his thirties, he could still be found digging for clues—but more often than not it was amidst the archives at the Public Library or in the Public Records room in Wampsville, New York. A pencil behind his ear and an oversized pair of black-rimmed glasses that perpetually slipped off his nose, he looked every bit the local historian that he was.

In the evenings, Danny often volunteered at Lorenzo, a museum and historic home of Cazenovia founder John Lincklaen. At the end of a long day of research, when his eyes were tired and his mind numb, he could relax among the chintz and china of an era accustomed to elegance and grace. It was during these cozy evenings at Lorenzo that he felt most at home, puttering amongst the belongings of people who had lived over two centuries ago and catching up with his co-volunteers about the comings and goings at the mansion.

These comfortable and often lively conversations almost always included a first-hand account of a ghostly encounter. At least weekly, one of his co-workers reported hearing footsteps going up the back stairs, dishes rattling in the kitchen as if someone were preparing afternoon tea, or drawers and doors that had been left firmly closed were found open. The stories were varied, and the ghosts that accounted for them seemed to show no particular preference in time or distinction in taste as to whom they would reveal themselves.

Except for Danny. For some reason, these elusive ghosts whom his co-volunteers had even come to know by name simply refused to reveal themselves to Danny. He was the only person who had never seen, heard, or even felt a darned thing. Generally an easy-going young man, he would be lying if he didn't say it bothered him. *Truly,* he thought to himself, *who could be more interested or more receptive to seeing a ghost than a historian? I mean, what could they possibly have against me?*

So determined to force these elusive friends' hands, he signed up for as many overnight shifts as he could in hopes of an encounter of some sort. But nothing ever happened, not even a tiny creak in the floors. He even spent the entire night one Halloween at the mansion, thinking that surely a departed soul or two would be lurking around on the most haunted night of the year.

Unfortunately, despite his fertile imagination, Danny spent another thoroughly uneventful night, and the following morning he begrudgingly gave up on his ghostly pursuits and resigned himself to learning about history the old fashioned way—through books and research.

That is until late one Thursday evening in December. It was one of those unexpected blizzards that arrived late in the afternoon dropping over two feet of heavy, white snow within hours. People left their workplaces early and returned home to an ongoing ticker tape on the bottom of their television screens issuing a severe storm warning for Madison County, a seemingly endless notification of closings and cancellations, and a stern warning to stay off the roads as the plows couldn't keep up with the snowfall.

But the visiting hours at the Lorenzo mansion were not included in the list of cancellations. Danny and his two co-workers, Sharon and Betsy, simply hadn't turned on the television or listened to the radio. Subsequently, they knew nothing of the storm, and by the time they looked out the windows it was too late to phone the local stations.

The chances of anyone showing up in the middle of a full-blown blizzard were slim, but not impossible. Danny had long ago learned that you could never be sure of anything when it came to Upstate New Yorkers and their storms. For many, a ban on all unnecessary travel was merely a challenge that sent every Tom, Dick, and Harry straight out to their trucks. So being the chivalrous fellow he was, Danny told the two ladies to go home and he would stick around until nine o'clock. His only plans for the evening were to go home and finish his book, and he could do that right here at Lorenzo.

By seven o'clock that evening, the stately mansion and its grounds were already swaddled in a two-foot blanket of velvety white snow. The boughs of the century old pines and furs that surrounded the estate looked like frosted Christmas cookies, and the dwarfed cottages like half eaten gingerbread houses. The driveway and sidewalk leading to the front door had been plowed earlier in the evening, but only a vague hollow in the snow remained. If some intrepid visitor were to dare come out that night, they might have seen the profile of Danny sitting under a dim light behind the two narrow paned windows that flanked either side of the great front door, his legs crossed, a book in his lap, and a pair of glasses perched precariously on the end of his nose.

So there Danny sat, reading his book and occasionally gazing out at the snow, which seemed to be subsiding a bit as the evening wore on. Other than the standing lamp beside him, the huge house was completely dark, and the snow that engulfed it made it eerily quiet. His hallway station was chilly, but he'd left his jacket on and felt quite comfortable.

Danny was so absorbed in his book that he was surprised to hear the old grandfather clock down the hall start its familiar calming chime. Danny checked his watch as he did every time the old clock rang. Force of habit, he guessed. Eight o'clock, another hour before he braved the roads. He happily returned to his book for another minute or so until he thought he noticed some movement outside on the front porch. He turned and peered over his glasses out the window. He was surprised to see two figures huddled together in the snow. It looked like a man and a woman. They were bundled up in long coats and hats, and had thick scarves wrapped around their jaws. Before he had a chance to get up and let them in, the man put his face up to the window, and cupping his gloved hands against the glass, looked in at Danny.

"Oh. Okay, hang on!" Danny spoke with a raised voice through the glass and gestured with his forefinger. Setting his book down, he stood up to get the keys that were in the pocket of his pants. "I'll be with you in a minute."

He rustled through one pocket, then the other until he finally found the keys. He saw the two figures huddled together patiently waiting for him. He shook his head and chuckled to himself as he struggled with the key. *One never knows, does one?* Finally, Danny opened the door.

An unexpected cold blast of air blew through the doorway and nearly sent him tumbling backwards into the hall. He braced himself and pulled his coat tighter around him with one hand while blocking the whirling snow with the other. "Come on in and get warm," he nearly shouted over the howling wind. "Did you run into trouble....."

Danny stopped short. He was stunned to see that no one was there and that the wind and snow had suddenly stopped. He stepped out onto the snow-covered porch and looked to see if maybe they had started to leave, but there was no one to be seen. At first he felt badly that maybe he hadn't opened the door in time, but that didn't make any sense. It had only been a matter of seconds. Where could they have gone so quickly? Completely perplexed, he walked out on the porch to take a look around, the cold snapping against his cheeks.

There were no footprints.

He looked to the left and to the right of the porch. Nothing. He looked down the long stairway up to the porch and each stop was covered with at least six inches of unbroken snow. *How the hell did they get up on the porch?*

Then he looked down and was shocked to see that the only footprints that broke through the drifts outside the doorway were his own. The sparkling snow on the porch, the stairs, and even the lawn was totally undisturbed. *Impossible!* Danny readjusted his glasses and walked first to one side of the porch then the other, but again there was no sign of the visitors. He stood in the cold, thoroughly bewildered, looking back and forth over and over again. But the landscape offered no explanation. It was silent except for the eerie sighs and groans of the pine trees, as if they had made it through another siege. He looked out at the lake. The night hung still over the whiteness of it, and a single star dangled innocently from above, his only witness to what he'd seen.

It was only then that it occurred to Danny that maybe he had finally seen a ghost—*two* of them, in fact! There could be no other explanation! *Is this what it felt like to see a ghost?* Had he finally connected with the mysterious history of the mansion? Perhaps they were travelers from the early days of Lorenzo, back in the eighteen hundreds, when people frequently sought refuge at the nearest home and were warmly received by a gracious host. Maybe for some reason, and just for that short time, Danny was given a glimpse of an evening that occurred during a different storm in another century.

Who they were and why they were there, he would never know, but suddenly his heart began to gallop inside his chest. He wasn't sure whether it was an attack of frenzied excitement or just plain fear, but he started to shake uncontrollably from head to foot. He didn't know what to do with himself. He couldn't wait to tell the girls, and considered calling them right then and there, but he also couldn't wait to get out of the mansion. He turned back into the house, closed and locked the front door. After absentmindedly pacing back and forth, he snatched his book from the chair, switched the light off, and fumbled his way through the darkness to the back door.

Once outside and after a short but desperate struggle with his quivering hands, Danny secured the lock. He then plowed his way through the snow to the white mound that had once been his car and, using the sleeve of his jacket, wiped off enough snow to open the door. He was still shaking like an idiot but told himself it was because he was freezing cold. Reaching in, he turned the ignition and switched the heat on full blast, then shut the door and went about cleaning off the rest of the car. By the time he was done, it was nice and warm inside. Like The Little Engine That Could, his car made its way through the snow-covered driveway and headed home.

Danny couldn't finish his book that night. He didn't even open it. Instead, he stayed up all night vacillating between trying to come up with a logical explanation for the events of the night and trying to calm his nerves. But after a whole night's deliberation, he came to the conclusion that there were no facts, fossils, or scientific research that could possibly account for it. And although it had taken a toll on his nervous system and he was very glad it was behind him, he was actually quite pleased to have finally seen through the curtain of time, to have experienced the unexplainable.

He would have his coffee in the morning, just like he did every other morning. And he would definitely get on the phone and tell Sharon and Betsy that he had finally seen a ghost. But that could wait. For now, just on the edge of a new day, Danny lay in his bed and looked out his window into the vast darkness. He was calm now; his nerves subdued. There was so much to learn, to research, so many fascinating layers to every facet of life. Danny had always proclaimed emphatically (to anyone who would listen) that the world was full of clues to the past. But what was the past, anyhow? Was it the same as the present? How about the future? Was time really happening all at once? He seemed to remember reading something about that several years ago.

Anyway, it was a wonderful new puzzle, something that definitely needed looking into. He smiled to himself. He had always wondered if a day might come when he wouldn't be curious anymore, wouldn't have some puzzle that needed solving. For some reason, he looked over at his too large glasses that were carelessly plopped on his bedside table.

"I don't think that's going to happen," he said out loud, "not anytime soon anyways." Then with a satisfied smiled on his face, he pulled the covers up close under his chin, closed his eyes, and fell fast asleep.

Chapter Eight

The Meadow

Tim's Story

It wasn't that unusual for eighteen-year-old Tim Smith to wake up at eight o'clock on a Saturday morning. What *was* unusual, in fact unheard of, was that he didn't roll over and go back to sleep till noon. But this October morning, when he looked out his window at the cobalt sky and cotton ball clouds, he had the unprecedented urge to get out of bed and be a part of the day. He got up and, trying to shake off the morning chill, hopped across the cold, bare floor to the window. The remaining dew sparkled in the sun like shattered crystal. It was one of those mornings where it would be warmer outside than it was in the house. He looked over at his 175-pound German Rottweiler that was stretched out like a human on the other side of his bed. "Hey, Imus," he whispered, "How about a walk, buddy?"

Imus looked up with sleepy eyes without even raising his head. He just looked as though he must have heard it wrong. Not because Tim didn't take him for walks, because he did. In fact, Tim and Imus knew just about every square inch of the trails in Chittenango Falls State Park. But never, ever did they walk this early on Saturday mornings.

Tim looked down at him and chuckled. "Yeah. You heard me right. Do you want to go for a walk or not?"

Imus cocked his big square head in bewilderment, and Tim couldn't think of anyone he loved more than that dog. "Come on, you big ox, let's go!"

Imus stood up and wagged his tail but, still not believing his ears, waited until he saw Tim climb into his sweatpants before he jumped off the bed and trotted to the door.

The kitchen was warm and smelled of fresh coffee. Tim's mother was padding around in her slippers and robe making the first quiet noises of a new day. When she saw Tim come lumbering in, she looked up at the clock.

"Well good morning! Isn't this kind of early for you to be up and about?"

Tim smiled patiently at his mom, then poured himself a glass of orange juice. "It's a beautiful morning, and Imus and I are going for a walk at the falls."

"Oh," she said, then adding under her breath, "your clock must be broken." Taking a sip of her coffee, she shuffled over to the kitchen table where the sun was most plentiful. Sitting down, she shook her head in the way that only a mother does. "Well then," she said seizing this rare opportunity, "maybe you can join us for breakfast when you get back!"

"Perfect!" Tim exclaimed, then gulped down the rest of his juice in two huge swallows. Her sarcasm was not lost on him one bit. He grabbed the leash, turned to his mother and said with exaggerated enthusiasm, "Sounds delightful, Mother Dear."

Chittenango Falls State Park was empty, just the way Tim liked it. He let Imus off the leash and let him run. "I guess we should come on Saturday mornings more often," he said, but Imus wasn't listening. He was already off exploring any new scents and smells since their last hike. The air was cool and moist, but not cold, and the sun felt like heaven on the back of Tim's neck.

They followed their usual route, down around the crashing waterfalls, through the campsite, and into the woods. The sound of the waterfalls faded, and all Tim could hear was the rustling echo of their feet brushing through the leaves. He looked up and couldn't see an inch of sky, only a tapestry of red, gold, and yellow that seemed to embrace him in its canopy of color.

They always took the Indian Trail. The marker warned of rugged hiking, but Tim and Imus climbed effortlessly over the rocks and fallen trees until they reached Tim's favorite spot. Those less familiar with the area might not even notice it, but about twenty yards off-trail to the north over a small rise was a huge horseshoe-shaped gorge with a dramatic eighty-foot drop. The tops of the trees that sprouted from its depths were lower than eye-level. Tim stood at the edge and breathed the silence deep into his belly. A little shower of pale yellow leaves floated aimlessly down into the uncharted darkness below. There was something about this spot that always seemed to peel back the layers of his soul. He liked to imagine that he was the only person that knew about it, that this amazing spot was his own little secret. Imus came up next to Tim and, knowing the routine, sat and waited.

After a time, Tim turned around and made his way back to the main trail. Then, just on a whim, he decided to explore a trail that he had never been on before. It was a path that his sister had mentioned a couple of weeks earlier. It led up a long, fairly steep hill to a meadow around the other side of the gorge that she told him was originally part of an Indian village. Imus looked puzzled for a moment then wagged his tail and trotted happily up the trail.

When they got to the top of the hill, the tunnel of woods opened up to a lush green meadow. The contrast in landscape was striking, almost as if someone had pulled a stage curtain and they'd entered into a different set. The trail that had been covered with colorful leaves became a clear, quiet, brown path surrounded by tall, sparkling grass. If it weren't for the telltale chickaree and goldenrod, it would have looked more like a fresh spring morning than the middle of October.

Tim keenly sensed how silent it was without the rustle of leaves underfoot and became aware of the sound of his breathing. Imus, on the other hand, trotted unawares ahead of him, his nose exploring the new scents and smells.

They were just short of the crest of the hill when Tim was surprised to hear the sound of children laughing over to his right. He couldn't see them over the tall grasses, but he immediately thought it was very odd because he hadn't seen a soul all morning. Besides, it had turned out to be quite a hike to get to this spot.

Imus heard it too. He immediately stopped dead in his tracks, sat back on his haunches, and perked his ears. Tim didn't pay him much heed and passed the Rottweiler, but stopped when he didn't hear the familiar panting resume beside him.

"Come on buddy, let's go."

But Imus sat motionless.

"Hey, come on Imus. Let's go see who's up there."

The dog didn't move a muscle, not even his eyes. This was completely out of character for Imus. The first thing Tim thought was that he must have somehow gotten hurt, stepped on something, and it was just a coincidence that it happened at the same time they heard the children. He walked back to Imus, playfully rubbed the scruff of his neck, and gave him a brief look-over. His baggy upper lip was caught on his right fang, but that was typical. Tim maneuvered the lip back in place and said, "Hey pal. What's the matter? Come on, it's just a couple of kids."

Imus flashed a quick, apologetic glance, but remained resolute. He wasn't budging. Frustrated now, Tim snapped the leash back on Imus' collar and tugged at it. "Come on Imus! That's enough. Let's go!"

But the 175-pound dog wouldn't budge.

"Okay, then." Tim shook his head and dropped the leash. "You stay here, you stubborn ox. I'm going to take a look."

But even as he said it, he knew Imus wasn't just being stubborn. Something weird was happening, and Tim felt a tickle of curiosity rise in his chest as he climbed to the top of the hill. He looked over toward where he'd heard the laughter.

There, about thirty yards off the trail, he saw three children, two girls and one boy. They were playing in the grass next to a heavy edge of woods. They were probably somewhere between four and six years old, the boy being the youngest. One of the girls had something in her hand, but Tim couldn't quite make out what it was. They giggled and chased each other around a group of three baby spruce trees, apparently enjoying the beautiful morning as only children can.

The little girls were clothed in dresses, and the boy wore shorts that fell just below his knees. As Tim got closer, he noticed their dark complexion and hair. There was something peculiar about the children and their clothing, but he couldn't put his finger on it. In fact, there was something about the whole scene that made Tim feel oddly like an interloper … like he didn't belong there … like he shouldn't even be seeing them. He looked back at Imus, who was still frozen where he stood.

"See, Imus?" He felt a little hypocritical even as he said it. "It's just a few kids. Come look!" He walked back to the dog and tugged the leash, but Imus kept his brawny bottom right where it was. There was no moving him.

It crossed Tim's mind that he really should head home because he was going to be late for breakfast. But that tickle had turned into an itch. Who were these children? Where were their parents? They had to be at least a mile from any house. He dropped the leash again, walked back to the crest of the hill, and again feeling like some strange intruder, peeked over for the second time.

They were gone. Even though he could still hear the giggling and laughter, they were nowhere in sight. He walked a little further, but all he saw were the three baby trees. Tim concluded that they must have wandered into the woods, so he shrugged his shoulders and turned to head home.

Suddenly, out of the corner of his eye, he saw movement in the woods, and the boy reappeared. Tim didn't see the girls, but could still hear their giggles behind the heavy boughs of pine. The little boy trotted in a couple of circles then, as unexpectedly as before, he disappeared into the woods again.

Tim couldn't say he saw the boy actually run into the woods. It was more like he suddenly wasn't there. What was even stranger was that at the very moment Tim lost sight of the boy, he lost the sound of the girls' voices as well. It wasn't like they had tired of their play, though ... it was more like someone had pushed a mute button.

Tim stood in the silence watching, listening, waiting, and hoping for some logical explanation. Could he have imagined the whole thing? If it had been like any other Saturday morning, if he'd stayed out till the wee hours, he might have considered that a strong possibility. But there wasn't a hangover within miles. There was no way to get rid of the feeling that he wasn't supposed to be there, that he wasn't part of the picture, that the strangest thing in his life had just happened.

• • •

When Tim and Imus walked through the kitchen door, the room was bustling with the final preparations for breakfast. Tim's mother, father, and two sisters maneuvered their way around the crowded room like a perfectly choreographed ballet. The smell of bacon and sausage made Tim realize how hungry he was. His mother was busy putting the last platters of food on the table when she looked up at him.

"Oh good! I was afraid you were going to miss breakfast. Pour the orange juice, will you? And warm up the syrup."

When everyone was finally seated and the clinking, clattering, and passing of dishes was complete, the conversation started.

"What are your plans for the day?"

"Where were you last night?"

"Did anyone catch the end of the movie?"

"Who took my ...?"

Tim's sister Laura nudged his shoulder and spoke softly. "How come you're so quiet this morning? Something wrong?"

Tim looked at her and realized he wasn't sure what to say. "No, nothing's wrong," he mumbled, his mouth full of pancakes. "I was just out walking Imus at the park, and I saw something kind of odd, that's all."

"So you saw the children in the meadow?"

Tim forced himself to swallow his mouthful before he choked on it. "Yeah? What do you mean? Have you seen them too?"

"Yeah." She looked at him with a self-satisfied smile then took a swig of orange juice. "Remember that day I told you to try that trail? Well, I'd seen them too, and it freaked me out. I knew they couldn't be real, because they were there one minute and gone the next."

"Why didn't you tell me what you saw?"

"Because I thought I had to be nuts. And you never would have believed me anyway. And … you of all people would *never* have let me forget it."

This is true, Tim thought to himself.

"So I wanted you to go and see if you saw anything weird up there," Laura continued. "What I *didn't* want was for you to be looking for it."

Tim nodded his head. Sometimes his sister amazed him.

She continued, maybe a little smugly. "Was it two little girls and a boy?"

Tim nodded again and said, "And they had on sort of old fashioned clothes."

"Of course they did, dummy! They were from a different century! Remember, that whole area was an Indian village."

Laura continued to describe the children perfectly—their clothing, their dark hair, and their playful demeanor.

"And did the little girl have flowers in her hand?"

"It was flowers?" Tim's mind was going in fast-forward, trying to catch up as Laura described in detail precisely what he had seen and in the exact spot where he had seen it.

Tim spent the rest of the day thinking about what he'd experienced on that morning walk, musing on the mysteries of life, death, and time as we know it. He felt unsettled. He had never been a believer in ghosts, he wasn't even sure there was an afterlife at all. In fact, he had recently come to fancy himself a persuasive advocate of atheism.

So now what was he supposed to do?

Later that night, he climbed into bed with Imus right behind him. He had left the window open just a bit, and there was a quiet, comfortable chill in the air. Within moments he could here Imus' breathing grow long and deep. The poor guy was exhausted. Tim knew he would never forget that morning walk. He was pretty sure that Imus wouldn't either.

He chuckled to himself at what an unusual day it had been for both of them. If he hadn't stayed home last night and gotten up early, he would never have seen the children, nor would he have to rethink everything.

None of it made any sense at all. The only thing he knew for sure was that he saw something that defied all logic. Was Laura right, and for some reason his life had been spliced into a beautiful October morning that had taken place over a century ago? He would have to rethink this all over again tomorrow. Right now he could barely keep his eyes open.

Tim reached for Imus and stroked his ears. He pictured the three little children, so happy and carefree, playing in the tall grass. He pictured Imus stubbornly refusing to look at what he already knew was unnatural.

"You're a good boy, Imus," he whispered between yawns. "Do you want to see if they will be there next Saturday?"

Chapter Nine

An Unexpected Guest

Robyn's Story

Only eight more days till Halloween, and it had been a long countdown. It was costume-shopping day, a newly formed annual event that had only started last year but had already become a favorite. It included lunch as well as shopping, and if two year old Rob and four and a half year old Tony weren't behaving like over-stimulated monsters by then, they would stop for pumpkins on the way home. It was a perfect day for it too. The air was crisp, the sky was clear and blue, and the trees were at their peak of color.

Robyn had just finished buckling the two boys in the back of her mother's brand new Saab, when her mother pulled two small paper bags with orange ribbons out of her pocketbook. She handed one to each of the boys and winked at Robyn over the top of the seat. "I thought this might be another nice tradition we could start?"

Robyn watched their eyes grow wide as they each reached in and pulled out a homemade powdered donut and a little carton of apple cider. She shook her head, closed the back door, and slid into the passenger seat next to her mother. "That, mother," she said, "is going to be one tradition you're going to wish you hadn't started."

"Why?" Her mother asked with a noncommittal look that sometimes accompanied her 'I raised you didn't I?' speech. "Too much sugar?"

Robyn looked at her mother. "Well yes, I guess you could say that...." She paused then nodded her head toward the back of the car. She didn't have to look to know that the entire back seat would be covered in white powder. She watched as her mother's expression changed from Dr. Jekyll to Mrs. Hyde.

"Oh no. Your father's going to kill me."

Robyn's mother was an intelligent, levelheaded woman who was no more afraid of Robyn's father as she was anything else. But sometimes she liked to pretend she was. Avoiding Robyn's eyes, she turned back around and buckled her seatbelt, then started the car.

"You're right," she finally conceded, "next time, I'll have to get a tarp."

A contented silence followed as the four travelers rounded the end of the lake and headed for the largest costume store in the city. The boys were happy with their donuts and cider. Robyn and her mom just soaked in the sheer beauty of an Upstate October day.

After he was done with his snack and probably because he was feeling the mood of the season, Tony, the oldest, said as innocently as any child might, "Mom, will you tell us the ghost story?"

Robyn was silent. His question wouldn't have been a problem at all except that the ghost story to which he referred was a true one— one that she had never told her mother. Robyn knew her mom didn't believe in ghosts. Not only that, but she knew she seriously questioned the sanity of anyone who did. Even that wouldn't have been a problem except that it was the story of an encounter that had happened to Robyn over twenty-five years ago, one that in all those years and for reasons she couldn't explain, she had never told a soul.

She glanced over at her mother, who returned her look with questioning eyes. There was also the tiny little detail that the ghostly encounter had occurred at an unknown and unsanctioned party at Robyn's parents' house. All in all, that encounter over two decades ago had been too weird, too incomprehensible, and too self-incriminating to even think of trying to explain it to anyone.

"Come on, mom," said Tony's little brother. "Tell us your ghost story."

Her mother, who was keeping a respectful silence, responded with one carefully raised eyebrow.

"*Come on mom!*" the boys said in unison.

"Okay, okay!" Robyn chided, then under a deep breath she sighed, "Might as well. It was a Friday afternoon in late November and it was already getting dark."

She looked out the car window at the spray of gold and burgundy foliage that crowned the hills around them. It so reminded her of that day.

"My best friend Meggie and I were walking to her house after tennis practice," she began. "All the leaves had fallen to the ground, and the trees were bare. I remember it so clearly because there had been a huge wind storm the night before, and the neat little piles of leaves that people had raked were blown all over the streets and sidewalks."

Robyn could see in her mind's eye the two of them kicking their way through the leaves with their schoolbooks and tennis rackets hugged tightly to their chests. *We were good kids*, she thought to herself. But sixteen year old girls are like the autumn leaves. Once they are free of the tree, they can fall prey to the whims of a breeze.

"Nanya and Grampa were out of town for the weekend, so Meggie was going to spend the night at our house. And ... well ...," she paused and glanced over at her mother, "we decided to have a couple of people over."

Though the two boys were too young to realize the significance of this statement, her mother did. But, keeping her eyes on the road, she squeezed her eyes semi good-naturedly.

"It was dark by the time we got to Meggie's, so her mom drove us to my house. I remember it seemed so quiet when we got out of the car, and the maples that lined the lawn looked huge and even darker than the sky. Inside, the house was pitch black. We'd forgotten to leave the lights on in the morning.

"Anyway, Meggie and I turned on the lights and got the house ready for our friends. Everyone arrived at about seven or so and we spent the evening playing twister, listening to music, and having pillow fights."

Her mother shot her a knowing glance.

"Soooooo," Robyn continued, "It was well after midnight before we finally got tired and decided to go to bed. Meggie and I cleaned up in the kitchen while everyone else got their sleeping bags out and set up camp in the living room. We had planned to sleep with the rest of them, but by the time we had finished in the kitchen, everyone had already fallen asleep.

"We weren't quite ready for sleep yet, and the idea of two nice beds seemed a lot more appealing than a cold, crowded floor. So we carefully maneuvered our way around the sacks of bodies and snuck downstairs to my bedroom. We got into our pajamas, climbed into our respective beds, and snuggled in for one last chat."

Robyn turned to her mother, "Do you remember the twin beds in my old room Mom? One was actually a trundle bed that you could pull out?"

Her mother thought about it, then said, "Oh yeah, I do remember that. So the beds were adjacent to each other."

"Yeah," Robyn nodded and put her hands in the shape of an L. "So our heads were right next to each other."

"That's right," her mother nodded.

"Well, so we got in bed and chatted about this and that. The moon must have risen but it wasn't full, because I remember there was just a hint of light coming in my window. We were sleepier than we thought, and it wasn't long before the spaces in between our conversation grew longer and longer. Eventually, I could feel myself drifting off to sleep.

"You know mom, how when you're just about to fall asleep? How sometimes you open your eyes just for a second without really meaning to? I don't know. It's weird, kind of like an unconscious reluctance to let go of the day?"

Her mother thought about it and nodded, "Actually yes, I know exactly what you mean."

"Well, like I have a million times before, I opened my eyes, expecting to just stare blankly at my room for a moment before closing them a final time. But this time, in that split second, I saw a man.

"He was over by my desk, not six feet away from me. At first I thought I must have already fallen asleep and was dreaming. I instinctively closed my eyes for a second or two, then looked again. But he was still there, not sitting, but kind of leaning against the desk next to the window. And the creepiest thing was that he held a lit cigarette between his thumb and his forefinger.

"I remember I blinked again and again, trying to wake myself up. But he was still there every time I looked, just casually raising the cigarette up to his lips, then down again as he inhaled deeply and blew a stream of smoke out of the side of his mouth."

Robyn tried to shake off the icy chill she was feeling. "I'll never forget the utter terror I felt at that moment. I remember thinking, *this is my room! I can't run anywhere!*

"At first I thought he was an intruder, but only for a second, because it didn't make sense. He was looking toward us but not at us, like he didn't even see us. And the weirdest thing was that I couldn't smell the smoke from his cigarette. *This has to be a dream*, I thought. But it wasn't. Was I hallucinating? I didn't know. All I knew was *there was no way out.*

"'Meggie!' I whispered, so quietly that even I could hardly hear it.

"'I see him,' she whispered back.

"I don't know what I wanted Meggie to say or do, but now I was even more terrified than before. If Meggie could see him too, that meant he was real! But he couldn't be! Something was terribly wrong. Was I having a dream, and for some bizarre reason Meggie was sharing it?

"'Do you see the cigarette?' I whispered.

"'Yes.'

"I could tell by her voice that she was as frightened as I was, and we both stared breathlessly at the red glow of the cigarette rising and falling with each slow, deliberate pull. I had an agonizing feeling of being trapped in another dimension of time and space, like two different moments in time were colliding.

"I wanted to turn the lights on, but the switch was all the way across the room, and I would have had to cross right in front of him. All of a sudden I felt like my insides were going to explode right through my skin, and with each excruciating moment the feeling intensified until I couldn't endure another second.

"Without thinking anything other than that this horrible encounter had to end, I jumped out of bed, raced right in front of the man over to the light switch, and flicked it on. Both the man and his cigarette were gone."

A satisfied silence filled the car as Robyn brought herself back to the present. Her heart was racing a bit. It happened every time she thought of it.

"Oooooh," mumbled Rob.

"That's sooooooo creepy Mom," said Tony.

"So what happened after that?"

Robyn was surprised to see that her mother not only seemed to believe her story, but also was truly interested.

"Well, nothing really," she said. "Meggie and I stayed up all night. There was no way we could sleep. We compared our versions of what we saw and everything matched exactly. We tried to find some sort of explanation, but never could. By the time the sun came up, we had made a pact—a pact that needed no argument or persuasion on either side. We agreed that the whole thing was just too weird, too unbelievable, and too disturbing to ever be repeated. It was almost like it upset both of us so much, we never even wanted to think about it again. And I don't know about Meggie, but I've never spoken a word of it to anyone until last year, when I told the boys."

"Hmm," her mother's eyes narrowed. "So is that why you moved to the upstairs bedroom?"

"Yup," Robyn nodded.

"Don't blame you one bit." She shook her head. "What did the man look like?"

"Oh my God, I'll never forget what he looked like. He was older, maybe late fifties or early sixties. He was kind of short, five foot seven or so. But he was strong, trim, and in really good shape. Kind of like a contractor. I remember he had on a pair of dirty jeans, big heavy work boots, and a well-worn plaid flannel shirt. His face was unshaven, and his hair was cut close to his head in a military-style brush cut. He wasn't scary necessarily. I guess *intense* would be the word."

"Oh! Oh! Oh!" Her mother slapped the steering wheel with her hand. "That's the builder!"

Robyn turned to her mother and thought she must have misheard her. "What did you say?"

"I said that it had to have been the German builder, Fred … oh, what was his last name? He's the one who built the house for my parents back in the fifties. You described him perfectly!"

Robyn couldn't believe her ears. Was she really going to have some sort of answer to the questions that had haunted her for over twenty years? And was it actually going to come from her mother?

"Yes!" Her mother said excitedly. "Fred … oh never mind. He built both our house in Dewitt and the one you grew up in. He was painstakingly scrupulous about his work and actually rather obsessive. And you're right; intense is the perfect word for him. He would go back and check on a house for years after he had finished it. It would be just like him to come and check on our house … even after he was dead."

Robyn was stunned. She couldn't believe her ears. But after a flurry of comparing information with her mother, it all made sense. She felt a huge sense of validation, and was glad that she could actually put a name to the smoking specter that visited her bedroom so many years ago. She would have to call Meggie tonight and tell her.

But as they drove on in silence, Robyn looked out at the leaves again. There was something about that last wild burst of color before the surrender to winter that always inspired a certain melancholy. She realized that she would never really be able to find the answers she needed. The fact that one night so long ago they had somehow been able to see into another dimension of a total stranger's life still inspired more questions than answers.

The car stopped at a red light. Two teenage girls were crossing the street–their backpacks swung over their shoulders, and their jeans cut so low, they looked like they were going to fall down. Given the time of day, they were probably either coming home for lunch or cutting class. One of them had a short spiked hairdo and the other had long blond hair with streaks of maroon. Robyn smiled to herself and thought of Meggie and herself so many years ago. The hair and clothes might be different, but teenage girls were still the same.

A single moment in time, she thought–so fleeting yet permanent, overlooked but never forgotten, so subtle yet so haunting. The contradictions didn't seem to confuse her as much right now, they didn't frighten her. She turned and looked at the two messes in the back seat that she called sons and felt a sudden surge of gratitude.

"Ok guys!" she said with gusto, "so what do you want to be this Halloween?"

Without a moment's hesitation both boys shouted in unison, "A ghost!"

CPSIA information can be obtained at www.ICGtesting.com

227339LV00001B/1/P